Okudzhava Bilingual

Edited by Olga Kuzmina

Originally published as issue #31 of the journal *Chtenia*.

Cover photo: Bulat Okudzhava.

ISBN 978-1-880100-26-4

StoryWorkz, Inc.
73 Main Street, Suite 402
Montpelier, VT 05602
storyworkz.com

Bulat Okudzhava

Poems

Contents

** All poems in these sections by Bulat Okudzhava, introduced by the curators.*

Bulat Okudzhava: An Appreciation[1]

Vladimir Kovner

Bulat Shalovich Okudzhava, who, in addition to the songs that made him famous, wrote poems, fiction and plays, was born in Moscow on May 9, 1924, into a family of active party members. His father was Georgian, his mother Armenian. In 1937, his father was executed and his mother incarcerated in the Karagandin Labor Camp. In 1942, 17-year-old Bulat volunteered for the Red Army and was sent to the front, where he was wounded several times. After the war ended, he graduated with a degree in literature from Tbilisi University and was sent to work as a teacher in a village near Kaluga. It was there he began to write. In 1956 he moved back to Moscow, where three years later he would publish his first collection of poems, entitled "Lyrics" – although the earliest poem in that collection, "With wild and willful flames, / Burn on, oh, fire, burn!" had been written more than a decade earlier, in 1946.

In the late 1950s, Okudzhava began to perform his verses in song for his friends, accompanying his singing with a guitar. Thus began

----

1. We would like to express our sincere appreciation to Vladimir Frumkin for the invaluable advice about producing this volume, as well as granting permission to use quotations from the two volumes of *Songs of Bulat Okudzhava*.

the highly influential era of the Russian "bards," which Okudzhava is considered to have fathered. His songs, which would eventually become immensely popular, were initially performed in private homes and circulated exclusively through "homemade" tape recordings. His first professionally produced record was issued in Paris, only in 1968. In 1961, his first short story, "Be Well, Scholar," was published in the famous collection *Tarusskiye Pages*. Despite continual persecution by the Soviet government and outrageous attacks from the state-controlled media and literary establishment, Okudzhava remained an honorable, principled writer and human being throughout his life.

This is the bare outline of his life. What is left out is his poetry, his music and his guitar.

And you cannot read poetry with your eyes alone; poems are created to be listened to, and therefore read aloud. Even if we read them silently, we hear them in our heads. The poetry of Okudzhava always sings; his poems are music itself.

Okudzhava's musicality, the defining feature of his poetry, has three aspects. The first is that he heard music everywhere, emanating from city courtyards, architectural ensembles and park fences, on the nighttime streets of Moscow, and in the interlacing of birch twigs. Second, Okudzhava constantly and naturally incorporated the most diverse musical instruments and terms into his poetry, ranging from guitars, horns, drums, flutes and clarinets to waltzes, marches, and so on. And finally, he possessed a remarkable musical ear. Even poems that for one reason or another were not set to music, beg to be sung.

The song "Leningrad Music" is an ideal example of all three aspects of Okudzhava's musicality. Anyone who has every visited Leningrad (or modern-day St. Petersburg) would certainly have seen the Winter Palace, the Admiralty and Rossi Street, the latter named after the Italian architect Carlo Rossi, one of the reigning masters of European-style architecture in Russia. Okudzhava was not only impressed by the visual

beauty of these locations, but he heard the combined scenery as music:

Enjoy carefree midnight but pin all your hopes on the morning,
When prayer's lost its power to wash away sin, guilt and woe.
The Admiralty's needle swoops downward without any warning
And pierces the heart, so the weariest blood starts to flow.

There is no parade that would merit such special fanfare.
It's played just for us, who emerge in the dawn from our homes.
From granite and ironwork harmonies swell everywhere
And Rossi Street sings to the music of iron and stone.

Like the Admiralty Needle in "Leningrad Music," Okudzhava's songs found their way into his audience's hearts, becoming a part of them for the rest of their lives. This is why Vladimir Frumkin, a musicologist, Okudzhava expert and performer of his songs, once noted that "Bulat was able so easily to clear from his path (and ours) the so-called mass Soviet songs and to open a new world for us, a world of songs accompanied (only) by guitar, celebrating goodness, love and the music of life."

It is worth noting that Okudzhava had no formal musical education, and could neither read nor write music. While performing he endlessly improvised, replacing words, varying the melody, rhythm and tempo of accompaniment, and in the words of Frumkin, "forming, as it were, different 'versions' of a song."

Okudzhava was not just a brilliant songwriter – he was one in a series of great Russian poets who, since Pushkin, have captured the love and imaginations of more than one generation of Russians. Before his first performance at the Leningrad House of Art, Okudzhava said to Alexander Volodin (the playwright and poet scheduled to introduce him): "Don't call [my works] songs. I am a poet. They are poems."

Volodin would later comment: "At one time poets were known as singers... If this word were not so old-fashioned, then, following the

French term *chansonnier*, Okudzhava ought to have been called a singer. But another term came into use, one that meant the same thing, but with something added, something important to everyone and personal to many. This new term was simply 'Bulat.' He was referred to by this name not only by his friends, but by everyone to whom he became an essential part of life... Every word in his songs is pure and exact, and never crowds the words surrounding it; his words are not empty sounds; each one knows its own worth and knows that it deserves to be considered poetry, even better than mere poetry. It is a word of a song, and on its little wings it has to fly over an enormous country."

Bulat entered my own life in 1959, at a time when he was almost unknown. Before his death, in 1997, I would attend many official and even more unofficial concerts, record his songs, and, like many of his admirers, distribute them throughout the world. In 1976, I contributed to the creation of a seminal four-volume (not to mention 40-cassette) collection, "The Songs of the Russian Bards," released in Paris by YMCA Press, that covered the works not only of Okudzhava but of other Russian bards, including the two other pillars of the Russian bard movement: Alexander Galich and Vladimir Vysotsky.

As early as 1965, Bulat's good friend Vladimir Frumkin conceived the idea of getting a Soviet publishing house to print the first book of sheet music for Bulat's songs. For seven years, they struggled fruitlessly. Frumkin would explain afterwards that to publish Okudzhava's music in its original form "would have meant officially acknowledging a dubious genre, one that had arisen in a disturbing manner, without any official planning, bypassing government approval and regulations through which songs were composed, selected and distributed in the Soviet Union... Before Okudzhava came along, the state's monopoly on songs seemed unshakable."

Their dream came true only in America: in 1980, Ardis Press published *65 Songs of Bulat Okudzhava*, compiled and designed with musical arrangements by Frumkin and lavishly illustrated with photographs, including some from my personal collection. The songs were translated

into English by Eve Shapiro. Bulat's second book of 28 songs was published in 1986, arranged by Frumkin, and this time translated by Tanya Wolfson.

In total, Okudzhava wrote approximately 800 poems, close to 200 songs, five novels, a number of short stories and two screenplays, as well as appearing in eight films. And now in Moscow, on the Arbat – which he referred to as his true home – there is a monument to Okudzhava, portraying the central image of his remarkable song (see page 28 for the full poem):

For the love that you give there's no known remedy
Though a thousand new streets, I chance to befriend.
Oh Arbat, my Arbat, my homeland, you'll ever be.
For my journey on you will not ever end.

A Note on the Translations

The curators have endeavored to make sure that the song translations contained in this issue are singable in English; that not only are they metrically identical to the Russian original, but that the words can be naturally sung in English in a way that is as close as possible to the pace and intonation with which Okudzhava performed them. The present selection of songs includes well-known works that have been translated by others, as well as works that are less known (undeservedly so, in our opinion), and which to our knowledge have never before been translated into singable form.

For the purposes of further acquainting readers with the main themes in Okudzhava's work, we have divided the poems into several sections that pertain primarily to subject matter. The lattermost section, irony, is Okudzhava's weapon of choice, and the pervasive tone in most of his poems. Love is a classifier of subject matter (with a number of subcategories included here, based on the object of his "loves"), but it is also a common attitude with which Okudzhava addresses his subjects. It goes without saying that many of the poems included here embody more than one of these categories.

– Lydia Stone

Contributors

NATALIA GOGOLITSYNA was educated at the Herzen Institute in St. Petersburg and teaches translation and Russian at the University of Bristol, UK. She has a scholarly interest in the field of lexis and phraseology, with particular emphasis on non-equivalence. She is co-author, with Derek Offord, of the second, augmented edition of *Using Russian: A Guide to Contemporary Usage*, Cambridge University Press, and of *93 Untranslatable Russian Words*, by Russian Life Books.

VLADIMIR KOVNER is an engineer, a journalist, and an English<>Russian translator and editor, specializing in poetry, bard songs, ballet and idioms. He and Lydia Stone have been collaborating since 2005. Vladimir was an active participant in the bard movement and his article The Golden Age of "Magnitizdat" is a classic discussion of this era in Soviet history. He has contributed numerous articles to collections about Bulat Okudzhava, in addition to writing on other literary topics for books and journals in both Russian and English. He has also published two books of poetic translation *Приласкайте Льва* (Pet the lion), 2010, and Edward Lear. The complete limericks with drawings, a bilingual English-Russian book (2015). He and Lydia are completing work on an English-Russian idiom dictionary.

BULAT OKUDZHAVA (1924-1997) was Georgian by nationality, but was born in Moscow and lived there nearly his entire life. A prolific composer of "author's songs" (*avtorskiye pesni*), his works were romantic and melodic, yet not overtly political. Still, his independent streak kept him from attaining official state sanction for much of his career and lead to his immense popularity among the Soviet intelligentsia, who widely distributed his recordings in *magnitizdat* form.

LYDIA RAZRAN STONE is a first generation American who works as a technical and literary translator from Russian into English. She earned a Ph.D. in Cognitive Psychology and spent 10 years working for NASA, tracking and writing about Soviet biomedical research relevant to space flight. Her first bilingual book of translations, a poetry collection by Irina Ratushinskaya entitled *Wind of the Journey*, was published in 2000 by Cornerstone Press. Many of her translations have been published in various venues and her translated plays have been performed. She is the editor of *SlavFile*, the publication of the Slavic Language Division of the American Translators Association, for which she writes a humor and cultural column. Her translation of Krylov's fairy tales, *The Frogs Who Begged for a Tsar* (and 61 other Russia fables by Ivan Krylov) was published by Russian Life Books, as was her translation of *The Little Humpbacked Horse* (by Alexander Ershov).

Love for Women

"Love is the theme of a large number of my poems and songs. For a long period of time we have virtually ceased to sing about love, and there was even felt to be something 'dubious' in the word 'woman' itself. As a protest against this falsity and prudish hypocrisy, I decided to be the first to sing in Russian the praises of Woman as an object of worship, to fall on my knees before her. I must confess that in so doing, I lost my sense of irony. If I directed it at anything, it was at myself as the hero of these songs, which expressed the helplessness and failure of men [in these situations]."

Okudzhava, like most male poets, wrote a number of poems addressing a traditional romantic subject – love for a woman. The two first poems included here, however, are far from traditional love poems. *"The gray of a late autumn sky are her eyes,"* sometimes known as "Behold How this Woman Loves Me," is an ironic anti-love poem, in which the unloved poet compares himself to a soldier standing at attention before a superior. The second, *"I feel the need for someone I can pray to,"* is more difficult to characterize. It breaks down naturally into three sections: 1)

the ironic and self-deprecating portrayal of the poet as an ant seeking a goddess to worship; 2) the arrival of the woman with all too human and sympathy-evoking physical details; and 3) the lyrical and truly romantic last stanza. This work can be described as a small *sui generis* masterpiece.

The *Sentimental March* is one of a rather large number of the poet's "love and war" poems, in which a soldier addresses a beloved woman at home. Hope is a strong theme in Okudzhava's works, and closely associated with love. The woman, who appears in a number of his poems, is called Nadezhda, which translates as hope.

The gray of a late autumn sky are her eyes,
Without any warmth I can see,
And I am oppressed by these ominous skies.
Behold how this woman loves me.

Goodbye. There's no way to go on. Let us part.
Each day it grows clearer to me:
All's empty inside and the future is dark.
Behold how this woman loves me.

It's time I went off, this I well understand,
To be self-respecting and free.
Old soldier I am; at attention I stand.
Behold how this woman loves me.

1959
Translation by Lydia Stone and Vladimir Kovner

I feel the need for someone I can pray to.
Imagine that a common lowly ant
Was overcome by yearning for a way to
Prostrate himself – as humble supplicant.

At peace no more, dispirited, frustrated,
So all the world appeared to him mundane,
A goddess in his image he created
And worshipped her; his prayers were not in vain.

For when his days of prayer had numbered seven,
She did appear to him one winter's night
Without a single augury from heaven.
The jacket that she wore was far too light.

Forgetting all the past – both pain and pleasure,
He opened wide the door out to the street
And kissed her hands chapped raw from wind and weather
And then the shabby slippers on her feet.

Two shadows moved like dancers in the entry
And wordlessly communion seemed to flow.
Oh, they were fair and wise like heaven's gentry,
But sad like mortal folk on Earth below.

1959
Translation by Lydia Stone and Vladimir Kovner

Глаза́, сло́вно не́ба осе́ннего свод,
и нет в э́том не́бе огня́,
и да́вит меня́ э́то не́бо и гнёт –
вот так она́ лю́бит меня́.

Проща́й. Расстаёмся. Поща́ды не жди!
Всё я́вственней день ото́ дня,
что пу́сто в груди́, что темно́ впереди́ –
вот так она́ лю́бит меня́.

Ах, мне бы уйти́ на доро́гу свою́,
досто́инство мо́лча храня́.
Но, ста́рый солда́т, я стою, как в строю́...
Вот так она́ лю́бит меня́.

1959

Мне ну́жно на кого́-нибу́дь моли́ться.
Поду́майте, просто́му муравью́
вдруг захоте́лось в но́женьки вали́ться,
пове́рить в очаро́ванность свою́!

И муравья́ тогда́ поко́й поки́нул,
все показа́лось бу́дничным ему́,
и мураве́й созда́л себе́ боги́ню
по о́бразу и ду́ху своему́.

И в день седьмо́й, в како́е-то мгнове́нье,
она́ возни́кла из ночны́х огне́й
без вся́кого небе́сного знаме́нья...
Пальти́шко бы́ло лёгкое на ней.

Все позабы́в – и ра́дости и му́ки,
он две́ри распахну́л в своё жильё
и целова́л обве́тренные ру́ки
и ста́ренькие ту́фельки её.

И те́ни их кача́лись на поро́ге.
Безмо́лвный разгово́р они́ вели́,
краси́вые и му́дрые, как бо́ги,
и гру́стные, как жи́тели земли́.

1959

Sentimental March

Nadezhda, Hope, I will come home
Soon as the bugler, elbow bended,
Up to his lips his bugle raises
And blows retreat for all to hear.
Nadezhda, I'll stay safe for you;
For me, war's grave was not intended.
What's meant for me is all your care,
The charmed world of your hope and fear.

But if a lifetime passes by
And of this endless hope you tire,
So it appears that I am destined
That death should hover over me.
Then bid that bugler to rise up,
Though he's been wounded under fire,
So that the last grenade of battle
Won't be the last thing that I see.

If suddenly the odds of war
And death I cannot keep defying,
There's sure to be some new world struggle.
For what and where, who can foresee?
No matter in what war I'm slain,
It's Russia's Civil War I'll die in
As Commissars in dusty helmets,
Unspeaking, stoop to peer at me.

1957
Translation by Lydia Stone and Vladimir Kovner

Сентимента́льный ма́рш

Наде́жда, я верну́сь тогда́,
когда́ труба́ч отбо́й сыгра́ет.
Когда́ трубу́ к губа́м прибли́зит и
о́стрый ло́коть отведёт.
Наде́жда, я оста́нусь цел,
не для меня́ земля́ сыра́я.
А для меня́ твои́ трево́ги,
и до́брый мир твои́х забо́т.

Но е́сли це́лый век пройдёт,
и ты наде́яться уста́нешь,
Наде́жда, е́сли на́до мно́ю
сме́рть распахнёт свои́ крыла́,
Ты прикажи́, пуска́й тогда́
труба́ч изра́ненный привста́нет,
Что́бы после́дняя грана́та меня́
прико́нчить не смогла́.

Но е́сли вдруг, когда́ нибудь,
мне убере́чься не уда́стся,
Како́е б но́вое сраже́нье
не покачну́ло б шар земно́й,
Я всё равно́ паду́ на той,
на той еди́нственной Гражда́нской,
И комисса́ры в пы́льных шле́мах
скло́нятся мо́лча на́до мной.

1957

Eternal Love
Bulat Okudzhava

When I was a very young man, I was astonishingly susceptible to falling in love. No, it's not what you're thinking; not a lack of discrimination in my affections, not lust, not the cold calculation of a male animal. This was a blazing fire, a kind of intoxication, a platonic madness. I truly fell in love. And when I would gaze upon the object of this love, I would grow wings and feel certain that this feeling was going to last from that moment on until eternity.

Of course, the relative superficiality characteristic of my age curtailed the duration of this fire. But while it lasted, I was absolutely sincere, faithful, generous, self-sacrificing, and happy. And all this would continue until another love object appeared.

When I met Alicia Boshyan, I felt something like an electric shock and understood that this feeling would last forever. Her predecessor immediately faded from my consciousness. And this effect did not depend on her beauty or any other specific qualities. Even then I was conscious that there was some kind of mysterious power controlling my infatuation. It would have been ridiculous to say, for example, that this girl's eyes were

ЛЮБО́ВЬ НАВЕ́КИ

Була́т Окуджа́ва

В ра́нней мо́лодости я был порази́тельно влю́бчив. Нет нет, э́то была́ не похотли́вость, не скло́нность к развра́ту, не холо́дная расчётливость самца́. Э́то был жа́ркий ого́нь, умопомраче́ние, платони́ческое безу́мие. Я влюбля́лся. И когда́ смотре́л на предме́т свое́й влюблённости, у меня́ выраста́ли кры́лья, и я понима́л, что отны́не э́то навсегда́.

Коне́чно, не́которое легкомы́слие, сво́йственное во́зрасту, определя́ло сте́пень э́того пожа́ра, но я был абсолю́тно поря́дочен, ве́рен, щедр, скло́нен к самопоже́ртвованию и сча́стлив.

И всё э́то до той поры́, пока́ не возника́ла друга́я.

Когда́ появи́лась Али́са Бошья́н, я вздро́гнул и по́нял, что э́то навсегда́. Её предше́ственница тотча́с поме́ркла. И де́ло тут бы́ло не в красоте́, не в осо́бых каки́х то досто́инствах. Я уже́ тогда́ сознава́л, что есть что то, кака́я то таи́нственная власть, утвержда́ющая моё восхище́ние. Смешно́ бы́ло бы говори́ть, что у э́той, наприме́р, глаза́ бы́ли прекра́снее, чем у той, и́ли что у э́той мане́ра обще́ния

more beautiful than that one's, or that one had a more enchanting manner than the other. Absolutely not, the chosen one was superior with regard to eyes, manner, nose, lips, and personality. And all this caused me to burn and to sincerely believe that I would feel this way eternally.

When Alicia Boshyan appeared, again I felt the electric shock and believed that I would love her for the rest of my life. She was beautiful, a tall, slender brunette with curls to her shoulders, green eyes and a mysterious smile.

She spoke very little, and this added to the mystery that gave me no peace. As a brunet myself, I tended to prefer blondes, but immediately blondes began to seem ordinary to me. I remember that I even felt astonished that some other man could choose to become infatuated with and to pursue some other girl, when this world contained Alicia.

At that time I was living in Tbilisi with my aunt. It was 1945. My aunt loved me very much and was a second mother to me. As a soldier who had only recently fought on the front lines, it was easy for me to gain admission to the university – and once there, many of my sins were forgiven. And there was much to forgive. I was not all that excited by my chosen subject of philology, but the thought that I had just returned from the front alive, and that, therefore, everything was permitted to me – and that my current love object could not take her eyes off me, and that in the evening she and I would walk together on the grounds of the Officers' House, and would dance the tango, foxtrot and Boston waltz – that thought excited me.

And so, only a few days after Alicia Boshyan appeared in my life and gave me an electric shock, I decided to introduce her to my aunt. I had brought all her predecessors home to aunty as well, and she had praised all of them ecstatically. It had become a tradition.

"I would like to introduce you to Alicia Boshyan," I said, filled with emotion.

"I am very glad to meet you," said my aunt. "He has told me so much about you with such admiration that I have been dying to meet you. And now, here you are!"

была́ обворожи́тельней. Нет нет, и глаза́ у той бы́ли прекра́сней, и мане́ра обще́ния, и нос, и гу́бы, и хара́ктер... А сгора́л от э́той и и́скренне ве́рил, что уж тепе́рь все, что э́то наве́ки.

Когда́ появи́лась Али́са Бошьян, я вздро́гнул. Она́ была́ прекра́сна. Высо́кая, стро́йная брюне́тка с ло́конами, покоя́щимися на плеча́х, с зелёными глаза́ми, с зага́дочной улы́бкой.

Она́ была́ немногосло́вна, и за э́тим то́же тайлось не́что, что не дава́ло поко́я. Я, как брюне́т, обы́чно был скло́нен к блонди́нкам, но тут все блонди́нки показа́лись заур́ядными. Я да́же, по́мню, удивля́лся, мол, как э́то мо́жно бы́ло име́ть де́ло с той и да́же е́ю восхища́ться и та́к обольща́ться на её счёт, когда́ в ми́ре существова́ла э́та!

Я жил тогда́ в Тбили́си у свое́й тёти. Шёл со́рок пя́тый год. Тётя меня́ о́чень люби́ла и была́ мне вме́сто ма́тери. Меня́, как вчера́шнего фронтовика́, легко́ при́няли в университе́т и мно́гое проща́ли. А проща́ть бы́ло что. Филоло́гия меня́ не о́чень возбужда́ла, но мы́сль о том, что я вчера́шний фронтови́к, что я жив, что мне в связи́ с э́тим все дозво́лено, что очередна́я па́ссия не сво́дит с меня́ глаз, что ве́чером мы пойдём с не́ю в парк До́ма офице́ров и бу́дем отбива́ть но́ги в та́нго, фокстро́те, в ва́льсе босто́не, — мы́сль об э́том о́чень возбужда́ла меня́.

И во́т появи́лась Али́са Бошьян, и я вздро́гнул и уже́ че́рез не́сколько дней реши́л познако́мить её с мое́й тётей. Всех предше́ственниц я то́же приводи́л к тёте, и всем она́ дава́ла са́мые возвы́шенные оце́нки. И э́то ста́ло тради́цией.

— Вот, — сказа́л я взволно́ванно, — знако́мьтесь, э́то Али́са Бошьян.

— Я о́чень ра́да, — сказа́ла тётя, — он сто́лько расска́зывал о вас, и с таки́м восхище́нием, что не терпе́лось познако́миться... О, вот вы кака́я! Ну, заходи́те, заходи́те, я о́чень ра́да...

The three of us sat down to supper. It was very romantic. My gaze meandered back and forth between Alicia and my aunt. The conversation was pleasant and natural. The Tbilisi evening air wafted in through the window. How wonderful that the war had ended!

It was rather late when I left to take Alicia home. And it was a rather long time after that before I returned home. I rushed into the apartment and accosted my aunt. She had been clearing the table.

"Well, what did you think?" I practically shouted at her. "Isn't she wonderful? I told you so! Weren't you charmed out of your mind? Weren't you? Weren't you?"

"Of course, of course," said my aunt, patting my head. "She is delightful! What a figure! What eyes!" She went into the kitchen and came back. "But, you know, of course I could be mistaken, but it seemed to me that her legs are a bit bowed." She immediately corrected what she had just said using the softening affectionate diminutive for "legs." Of course, I very well might be mistaken. And of course, such things do not matter a bit, do they?"

"Of course not," I hastened to reply.

I slept badly. I kept waking up and thinking about Alicia's legs. Why did my aunt have to even mention something so trivial?

I awoke in the morning and again thought about the same subject. I went to the university and ran into my fellow student, Katya Loman. She had slender legs. I looked around at the other female students. They all had lovely legs. I caught sight of Alicia approaching at the other end of the hallway. I examined her carefully; she was indeed bowlegged. Not very, but unmistakably. What's more, she had an awkward gait, as though she was walking on a slippery surface.

A week passed, and when we met, we only exchanged polite greetings. I nodded to her and, passing her by in the classroom, took a seat next to Katya. And gazing at her, I understood that this would be forever.

First published in Russian: 1997
Translation by Lydia Stone

Мы у́жинали втроём. Бы́ло о́чень серде́чно. Я смотре́л то на Али́су, то на тётю. Разгово́р был ми́лым и непринуждённым. Тбили́сский ве́чер вплыва́л в окно́. Как хорошо́, что зако́нчилась война́!

Уже́ бы́ло дово́льно по́здно, когда́ я отпра́вился провожа́ть Али́су. Верну́лся я не ско́ро.

Вбежа́л в кварти́ру, бро́сился к тёте. Она́ убира́ла со стола́.

— Ну что?! — почти́ закрича́л я. — Какова́, а? Я ведь говори́л!.. Ты ведь не разочарова́лась? Да? Да?..

— Ну что ты, — сказа́ла тётя и погла́дила меня́ по голове́, — она́ великоле́пна! Кака́я фигу́ра! А глаза́!.. — Ушла́ на ку́хню, верну́лась: — Да, кста́ти, мо́жет, коне́чно, мне показа́лось, но у неё немно́го криву́е но́ги... — и ту́т же попра́вилась: — но́жки... Впро́чем, мо́жет быть, и показа́лось... Да э́то, в су́щности, тако́й пустя́к... Не та́к ли?

— Коне́чно, — вы́дохнул я оторопе́ло.

Спал пло́хо. Просыпа́лся и ду́мал про но́ги Али́сы. Поду́маешь, ду́мал я, кака́я ме́лочь!

У́тром, просну́вшись, сно́ва поду́мал о том же. Прие́хал в университе́т, встре́тил свою́ соку́рсницу Ка́тю Ло́ман. У неё бы́ли точёные но́жки. Огляде́л остальны́х соку́рсниц. У всех бы́ли великоле́пные но́ги. В конце́ коридо́ра показа́лась Али́са. Прибли́зилась. Я отчётливо разгляде́л, что у неё ноги действи́тельно криву́е. Не о́чень, но криву́е. Да́ и похо́дка неуклю́жая и стра́нная, сло́вно она́ ступа́ет по ско́льзкому по́лу.

Че́рез неде́лю, встреча́ясь, мы про́сто здоро́вались, я, кивну́в, проходи́л ми́мо в аудито́рию и уса́живался ря́дом с Ка́тей и, огляде́в её, понима́л, что э́то наве́ки.

Love for Places

*The word "Arbatsvo" [approximately the qualities Arbat represents]
remarkably rhymes perfectly with the word "bratstvo" [Russian for
brotherhood] and, for me, stands for a set of qualities to which
I attach a great deal of importance. It defines my nature, my
psychology, my relationship to other people and my environment;
to my education and native soil...*

*The actual street of my youth was not a nice street... [I lived] on
Arbat Street itself at Number 43... in that old house... It was a large
and dirty courtyard, and has remained so – horribly dirty – and yet
trees grow there.*

Polytika, October 8, 1983

*My love for him (my city, i.e., Moscow) grows daily, it grows more
fierce each day; and, from this love, I fashion the gods to whom
I pray.*

From "My City Now is Drowsing," published in *Chtenia* 25

You, Moscow, in tears don't believe, and for this won't apologize.
Courageous and strong, iron city, you're staunch to the last.
From "The Past's Dead and Gone," published in *Chtenia* 25

[Okudzhava] became the guardian angel of [Moscow's] intelligentsia. He is a Muscovite three times over. It seems that without Bulat, neither the Moscow of sixties, nor the seventies, nor the eighties could have existed.
Russian dissident and journalist Valeriya Novodvorskaya,
on Bulat Okudzhava, *Medved* magazine, *147, 2011*

The love songs Okudzhava wrote to places are less ironic and closer to traditional love songs than the ones he dedicated to women. A favorite topic is Arbat, a street and district of Moscow where the poet lived as a child and returned to as a young man. Perhaps the most famous of these love songs is "Song about Arbat," which challenges the translator with its irregular meter and contrast between prosaic words and images (e.g., asphalt) and its ecstatic tone.

Okudzhava was essentially a poet of urban Russia and wrote relatively few major works about the beauties of nature – or, despite his Armenian/Georgian ancestry, about the scenic beauties of the then-Soviet Union. However, one of his most beautiful lyric love poems, the second in this section, is dedicated to the Black Sea.

Song about Arbat

Street with curious name! Asphalt river! How you gleam!
I see light shine though you, feel your currents flow.
Oh Arbat, my Arbat, you're my purpose, you're my dream.
You're my joy, my delight, yet you are my woe.

Oh, those walking on you – they're not high society –
Just plain folks who have tasks on my bustling street.
Oh Arbat, my Arbat, you're my faith, my piety.
And I am at my best when you're 'neath my feet.

For the love that you give there's no known remedy
Though a thousand new streets, I chance to befriend.
Oh Arbat, my Arbat, my homeland, you'll ever be.
For my journey on you will not ever end.

1959
Translation by Lydia Stone and Vladimir Kovner

Black Sea

Amidst waves – blue, free, irrepressible, here I stand.
They roll on, they roll on, unabating.
The Black Sea seems a goblet I hold in my hand
Filled with wine, like the waves, undulating.

There's one thought, one thought flowing now through my mind,
As if all of my hopes I've forsaken.
Oh Black Sea, it's you that I toast with this wine,
And I drink, of your essence partaking.

There's no sea but you that my love can command.
How could I give you up without grieving?
Oh Black Sea, your waves lapping my open hand,
Moving off like a boat that is leaving.

1961
Translation by Lydia Stone and Vladimir Kovner

Пе́сенка об Арба́те

Ты течёшь, как река́. Стра́нное назва́ние!
И прозра́чен асфа́льт, как в реке́ вода́.
Ах, Арба́т, мой Арба́т, ты моё призва́ние.
Ты и ра́дость моя и моя беда́.

Пешехо́ды твои́ лю́ди невели́кие,
Каблучка́ми стуча́т по дела́м спеша́т.
Ах, Арба́т, мой Арба́т, ты моя рели́гия,
Мостовы́е твои́ подо́ мной лежа́т.

От любо́ви твое́й во́все не излечишься,
Со́рок ты́сяч други́х мостовы́х любя́.
Ах, Арба́т, мой Арба́т, ты моё оте́чество,
Никогда́ до конца́ не пройти́ тебя́!

1959

Мо́ре Чёрное

Непоко́рная голуба́я волна́
все бежи́т, все бежи́т, не конча́ется.
Мо́ре Чёрное, сло́вно ча́ша вина́,
на ладо́ни мое́й все кача́ется.

Я все ду́маю об одно́м, об одно́м,
сло́вно бе́рег наде́жды поки́нувши.
Мо́ре Чёрное, сло́вно ча́шу с вино́м,
пью во и́мя твоё, запроки́нувши.

Неизме́нное среди́ мно́гих море́й,
как расста́ться с тобо́й, не отча́яться?
Мо́ре Чёрное на ладо́ни мое́й,
Как барка́с уходя́щий кача́ется.

1961

With the composer Isaak Shvarts

Love for Life and Humanity

I long to see love occupy its rightful place in human society, which would prevent it from turning into a barracks and would give each individual the opportunity to develop in a way that is unique to that person. I long to see all traces of 'personality cults' disappear from the surface of my Earth, and for democratic principles to become the norm everywhere.

Love of life and humanity pervades this poet's work. It appears in many of his songs dedicated to art, and especially music, and is often joyous in tone. This is perhaps best exemplified by "Song of the Open Door," certainly one of the most cheerful and optimistic in Okudzhava's body of work. In general, however, Okudzhava's love of his fellow man is expressed with at least a strong element of sadness and pity for the suffering of humanity, as in the second poem in this section, "*To shouts of a crowd demonstrating.*"

Song of the Open Door

Oh, when outside the storm winds roar
So loud they'd wake the dead,
Then do not rush to slam your door,
But open it instead.

And if you leave your home for long
To travel wide and far,
Do not forget this little song:
Please leave your door ajar.

And when at night you venture forth,
I hope you'll be inspired
To make a fire in the hearth,
To mix with your heart's fire.

Let cozy rooms and fire's glow
Call out to all who pass.
Closed doors aren't worth a damn, you know
Locks' value? Even less.

1959

Translation by Lydia Stone and Vladimir Kovner

Пе́сенка об откры́той две́ри

Когда́ мете́ль кричи́т, как зве́рь –
Протя́жно и серди́то,
Не запира́йте ва́шу две́рь,
Пу́сть бу́дет две́рь откры́та.

И е́сли ля́жет да́льний пу́ть
Нелёгкий пу́ть, предста́вьте,
Две́рь не забу́дьте распахну́ть,
Откры́той две́рь оста́вьте.

И, уходя́ в ночно́й тиши́,
Без ли́шних слов реша́йте:
Ого́нь сосны́ с огнём души́
В печи́ перемеша́йте.

Пу́сть бу́дет тёплою стена́
И мя́гкою – скаме́йка...
Дверя́м закры́тым – грош цена́,
Замку́ цена́ – копе́йка!

1959

To shouts of a crowd demonstrating
That threatens and calls Jews a blight,
The very last Jew emigrating
In the train station turns out the light.

The streams of insults, imprecations
He waves off with hand gaunt and white.
The fear-ravaged face of his nation
Peers out as the train moves from sight.

As if from the depths of humanity,
He looks at the past near and far.
And his birthland flows past all too rapidly
This last olive-green railroad car.

These days, when the whole world is churning
And changing the fate of mankind,
The Jew who for Russia keeps yearning
Weighs hard on this conscience of mine.

1989
Translation by Lydia Stone and Vladimir Kovner

Под кри́ки толпы́ угрожа́ющей,
хрипя́щей и сто́нущей вслед,
после́дний евре́й уезжа́ющий
пога́сит на ста́нции свет.

Пото́ки прокля́тий и ру́гани
худо́ю руко́ю стряхнёт,
и ме́дленно про́филь испу́ганный
за тёмным стекло́м проплывёт.

Как бу́дто из недр челове́чества
гляди́т на мину́вшее он...
И ка́тится ми́мо оте́чества
после́дний зелёный ваго́н.

Весь мир, на́ши су́дьбы тасу́ющий,
гуди́т средь лесо́в и море́й...
Евре́й, о Росси́и тоску́ющий,
на со́вести го́рькой мое́й.

1989

The Mouse
Bulat Okudzhava

One winter evening I was sitting in Peredelkino watching television. Suddenly a mouse emerged from under the sofa and sat at my feet. I cried out in disgust and she disappeared under the sofa.

My peace of mind was shattered. I remembered last year's mouse invasion, how I had abandoned everything else I had to do and instead spent my time setting mousetraps, sprinkling the floor with poisoned grain, tossing little gray corpses out into the snow, hiding food that I was too squeamish to touch. And despite all this, they continued to commit outrages. Their numbers grew and grew. They scurried over the blinds, squeaked, left their disgusting traces everywhere and multiplied behind the bookcase, so that their pinkish progeny from time to time crawled out into the open to get a look at the greater world.

Things continued this way for a month. I eventually sighed and gave up. Suddenly they disappeared. A specialist in such matters explained that it had been a special banner year for mice.

And now, was it starting again?

МЫ́ШКА

Була́т Окуджа́ва

Одна́жды зи́мним ве́чером я сиде́л в Переде́лкино у телеви́зора. Вдруг из под дива́на вы́шла мышь и усе́лась у мое́й ноги́. Я закрича́л с отвраще́нием, и она́ исче́зла под дива́ном.

Поко́й ру́хнул. Я вспо́мнил прошлого́днее наше́ствие мыше́й, как я, забро́сив все дела, расставля́л мышело́вки, рассыпа́л отра́вленные зерна, выбра́сывал на снег се́рые тру́пики, пря́тал пищу, брёзговал к ней прикаса́ться... А они́ продолжа́ли бесчи́нствовать. Их станови́лось все бо́льше и бо́льше. Они́ вскара́бкивались по што́рам, пища́ли, повсю́ду оставля́ли свои́ отврати́тельные следы́ и плоди́лись за шка́фом, и ро́зовенькие их насле́дники вре́мя от вре́мени выполза́ли отту́да на свет бо́жий...

Так продолжа́лось с ме́сяц. Я вы́дохся, опусти́л руки. Вдруг они́ исче́зли. Специали́сты объясни́ли, что э́то был како́й то специфи́ческий мыши́ный год.

И во́т тепе́рь сно́ва?!

Я за́мер на дива́не, и она́ появи́лась сно́ва и сно́ва усе́лась у мое́й ноги́. Я шевельну́л ного́й – она́ исче́зла. Страх и отвраще́ние бушева́ли

I froze on the sofa, and the mouse appeared again and again, and sat at my feet. I moved my foot and she disappeared. Fear and disgust raged within me. I dragged the mousetrap out of the storeroom, set it, and placed it in a dark corner. Again my peace of mind was destroyed.

I slept badly. I saw no sign of her for the entire next day. But in the evening, I had barely time to seat myself in front of the TV, when she appeared. She sat at my feet with her back to me, and gazed steadily at the screen. I moved my foot – and she reluctantly moved away. I froze and she again emerged from under the sofa and sat in her former place. Strange as it might seem, I no longer felt disgust. On the contrary, a sort of interest, a sort of mild curiosity was awakened within me. What was going on? Why did she take this pose? What did she want?

I bent over to look at her more closely, but she scurried out of sight.

For several days, everything followed the previously established pattern. I gradually looked her over. She was pretty! Suddenly I understood that she was pretty. I saw her little black shining eyes and her elegant little nose, her light gray coat and expressive, pretzel-like tail. She got used to me. She gradually stopped disappearing under the sofa, and simply delicately moved away a bit when I moved.

I put a little piece of pastry on the floor. She ate it eagerly, wiped herself off with her tiny paw and again focused on the screen.

A month passed. There wasn't anything she hadn't been treated to, hadn't tasted: baked goods, lard, sausage. I had gotten used to her; more than that, I had gotten attached. Now it would have seemed strange to me to watch TV in my previous solitude. I do not know what she did during the day, but in the evening the screen lit up and she immediately sat herself down in front of it. And I was glad she did. I even ceased to be reminded of last year's herd of gray creatures, that rioting mob. I am not generally a lover of crowds. Thank God that, in my home at least, the rioting had ceased. But this tiny, elegant creature in the light gray fur coat evidently shared my taste for solitude and showed no signs of yearning for the company of her frenzied fellow rodents.

во мне. Я вытащил из чулана мышеловку, зарядил её и поставил в тёмном углу. Покоя снова не было.

Я плохо спал. Весь следующий день она не появлялась. Но вечером, едва я уселся перед телевизором, она возникла. Она сидела у моей ноги, спиной ко мне, и не отрываясь глядела на экран. Я шевельнул ногой – она нехотя удалилась. Я замер – она вышла из под дивана и уселась на прежнее место. Странно, но я уже не испытывал отвращения. Напротив, какой то интерес, какое то ненавязчивое любопытство проснулось во мне. Что это такое? Что за поза у неё? Чего она хочет?..

Я наклонился, чтобы к ней присмотреться, но она исчезла.

В течение следующих дней все совершалось по уже установившемуся распорядку. Я постепенно разглядел её. Она была хороша! Вдруг я понял, что она хороша. Я видел её маленькие сверкающие чёрные глазки и изысканную мордочку, и светло серую шубку, и выразительный хвостик кренделько́м. Она привыкала. Она постепенно перестала исчезать под диваном, а просто чуть чуть деликатно отодвигалась в сторону, стоило мне пошевелиться.

Я положил на пол кусочек печенья. Она его с аппетитом погрызла, утёрлась лапкой и вновь уставилась на экран.

Прошёл месяц. Чего только не испробовала она, чем только не лакомилась: и печеньем, и салом, и колбаской... Я привык к ней, мало того – привязался. Теперь было бы странно смотреть телевизор в прежнем одиночестве. Не знаю, чем она занималась днем, но вечером зажигался экран – и она тотчас усаживалась перед ним. Мне было хорошо. Я даже перестал вспоминать прошлогоднюю стаю серых животных, эту беснующуюся толпу.

Я вообще не любитель толп. Слава богу, что хоть у меня в доме они отбушевали. А это маленькое изящное существо в светло серой шубке тоже, видимо, склонно к уединению и вряд ли тоскует по своим сумато́шным соплеменникам...

During the day I would work at my desk as usual. In the winter it gets dark early. And the thought would come to me that soon I would turn on the TV and sit tête a tête with her.

Suddenly something snapped loudly. I looked around and saw that the mousetrap, which I had forgotten all about, had been triggered! I rushed over to it – and saw my mouse in its clutches.

Later, some friends came to visit and I told them this story. They all sat in dejected silence. Fazil cried out, "Don't tell me it killed her?!"

First published in Russian: 1996
Translation by Lydia Stone

Днем я, как всегда, рабо́тал за свои́м столо́м. Зимо́й темне́ет ра́но. Я поду́мал, что ско́ро включу́ телеви́зор и мы уся́демся с не́ю...

Вдруг что то гро́мко щёлкнуло. Присмотре́лся – а это срабо́тала мышело́вка, о кото́рой я успе́л позабы́ть! Ки́нулся к ней – а в ней моя́ мы́шка!..

Как то у меня́ сиде́ли друзья́. Я рассказа́л им э́ту исто́рию. Все удручённо замо́лкли. Фази́ль вскри́кнул: «Неуже́ли на́смерть?!»

War and its Aftermath

Sadness and irony, which are the characteristics of my mature writing, are mainly the result of the war. It is not surprising that my poems deal with war so often – and indeed, my first published prose piece was about war, as were both of the movie scripts I wrote. While at the front I understood my own weakness and became convinced that, although much depends on the striving and will of the individual, he nevertheless is dependent on external objective circumstances that force him to suffer and deny him happiness, sometimes even life itself. While fighting the war, I felt anger at the cruelty of fate, which stole so many people close to me without their having deserved this fate. But at the same time I learned the great art of forgiving and understanding.

* * *

War taught me not to be impressed by parades and not to attach importance to the wonderful music played by military orchestras, which belongs in musical comedies and operettas. The war is still not over for me, since I am still well aware of what sacrifices were made in its name.

Okudzhava volunteered for the Soviet Army and was sent to the front in 1941, at the age of 17, in the service of the same state that had executed his father and incarcerated his mother. In 1944 he was invalided out of military service, having lost whatever illusions he might have had about the glory of war, after seeing innumerable young men die and being wounded himself several times.

The first poem in this section, "*Forgive us foot soldiers,*" is a lyrical anti-war marching song with a beautiful image of spring. Note the irony of asking forgiveness on behalf of the foot soldiers, who are in no way responsible either for the actions described in the poem, nor for their own suffering. The second poem, "*You know, I somehow can't believe I really went to war,*" was written in the last decade of Okudzhava's life and emphasizes the contrast between what actually happens in war and what a "normal" human heart can accept. The irony in the very short third poem lies in the contrast between the tragedy that befalls the "young tadpoles" in war and the upbeat form of the poem, which resembles a folk tune or a children's song.

Forgive us foot soldiers for doing what seems an irrational thing:
We're always departing from places just starting to burst into Spring.
The pace is unsteady, but there's no escaping; do not even try.
Just white pussy willows, like white-clad young sisters, to wave you goodbye,
Just white pussy willows, like white-clad young sisters, to wave you goodbye.

Don't trust in the weather – cold rain may soak through you, although it is Spring.
Don't trust the foot soldiers, no matter what brave rousing songs they may sing.
Don't trust those who tell us that soon we'll again hear the nightingale's song.
Accounts won't be settled between life and death for who knows how long.
Accounts won't be settled between life and death for who knows how long.

One lesson we've learned here, that nothing on Earth but the marching is real.
Admit, comrade soldier, for men such a life on the march has appeal:
One foot, then the other. Yet we're kept awake nights by one troubling thing:
Where is it we're headed, when marching from places just bursting with Spring?
Where is it we're headed, when marching from places just bursting with Spring?

1961
Translation by Lydia Stone and Vladimir Kovner

Прости́те пехо́те, что́ так неразу́мна быва́ет она́.
Всегда́ мы ухо́дим, когда́ над Землёю бушу́ет весна́.
И ша́гом неве́рным, по ле́стничке ша́ткой, спасе́ния нет.
Лишь бе́лые ве́рбы, как бе́лые сёстры глядя́т тебе́ вслед.
Лишь бе́лые ве́рбы, как бе́лые сёстры глядя́т тебе́ вслед.

Не ве́рьте пого́де, когда́ затяжны́е дожди́ она́ льёт,
Не ве́рьте пехо́те, когда́ она́ бра́вые пе́сни поёт,
Не ве́рьте, не ве́рьте, когда́ по сада́м закрича́т соловьи́.
У жи́зни со сме́ртью ещё не око́нчены счёты свои́.
У жи́зни со сме́ртью ещё не око́нчены счёты свои́.

Нас вре́мя учи́ло, живи́ по прива́льному, дверь отворя́.
Това́рищ мужчи́на, как всё же зама́нчива до́лжность твоя́,
Всегда́ ты в похо́де, и то́лько одно́ отрыва́ет от сна —
Куда́ ж мы ухо́дим, когда́ за спино́ю бушу́ет весна́?..
Куда́ ж мы ухо́дим, когда́ за спино́ю бушу́ет весна́?..

1961

You know, I somehow can't believe I really went to war.
Perhaps I saw a picture once, the kind that school boys draw,
In which I stamped and waved my arms and raised an awful din
And felt quite sure I would survive and hoped that we would win.

You know, I somehow can't believe that I shot young men dead.
Perhaps 'twas just a film I saw or else a book I read.
And never did I grab my gun and cause a life to end,
And thus my hands are free of blood and my soul's unstained.

You know, I somehow can't believe that I lived through those years.
Perhaps I died and now reside above this vale of tears.
In Paradise, in snow-white garb, amidst fair groves and streams.
And this fine life we lead on Earth is just my nightly dream.

1987
Translation by Lydia Stone

Don't trust in war, young tadpole,
She is an evil flirt.
An evil flirt, young tadpole,
Like boots she'll pinch and hurt.

The dashing steeds you dream of
Can't do a thing for you,
To save you from the stream of
Gunfire aimed at you.

1959
Translation by Lydia Stone

Ах, что́-то мне не ве́рится, что я, брат, воева́л.
А мо́жет, э́то шко́льник меня́ нарисова́л:
Я ру́чками разма́хиваю, я но́жками сучу́,
И уцеле́ть рассчи́тываю, и победи́ть хочу́.

Ах, что́-то мне не ве́рится, что я, брат, убива́л.
А мо́жет, про́сто ве́чером в кино́ я побыва́л?
И не хвата́л ору́жия, чужу́ю жизнь круша́,
И ру́ки мои́ чи́стые, и пра́ведна душа́.

Ах, что́-то мне не ве́рится, что я не пал в бою́.
А мо́жет быть, подстре́ленный, давно́ живу́ в раю́,
И ку́щи там, и ро́щи там, и ку́дри по плеча́м...
А э́та жизнь прекра́сная лишь сни́тся по ноча́м.

1987

Не верь войне́, мальчи́шка,
не верь, она́ грустна́.
Она́ грустна́, мальчи́шка,
как сапоги́, тесна́.

Твои́ лихи́е ко́ни
не смо́гут ничего́.
Ты весь — как на ладо́ни,
все пу́ли — в одного́.

1959

Genius
Bulat Okudzhava

The events I am about to describe took place during one summer long before the war, when I was 12 and living with my aunt and uncle in Tbilisi.

Like almost all children and adolescents, I wrote poems. I found every one of them wonderful and would immediately read each new creation to my aunt and uncle, who were, to put it mildly, not great experts on poetry. My uncle worked as a bookkeeper and my aunt, though well educated, was a housewife. Nevertheless, they were extremely fond of me, and whenever I read them a new poem they ecstatically exclaimed, "Brilliant!" "He is a genius," my aunt would cry. And my uncle would enthusiastically agree: "No doubt about it, dear. A true genius!"

One day my uncle thought to ask me, "Why isn't there a single book of your poems? Pushkin has hundreds; so does Bezymensky. But there's not even one of yours."

That got me thinking. He was right, of course, not a single book! But why wasn't there? And this sad injustice so moved me, that I set off for the Writers Union Building on Machabeli Street.

Ге́ний

Була́т Окуджа́ва

Э́то бы́ло задо́лго до войны́. Ле́том. Я жил у тёти в Тбили́си. Мне бы́ло двена́дцать лет. Как почти́ все в де́тстве и о́трочестве, я попи́сывал стихи́. Ка́ждое стихотворе́ние каза́лось мне замеча́тельным. Я вся́кий ра́з чита́л вновь напи́санное дя́де и тёте. В поэ́зии они́ бы́ли не сли́шком све́дущи, что́бы не сказа́ть бо́льше. Дя́дя рабо́тал бухга́лтером, тётя была́ просвещённая домохозя́йка. Но они́ о́чень меня́ люби́ли и вся́кий ра́з, прослу́шав но́вое стихотворе́ние, восто́рженно восклица́ли: «Гениа́льно!»

Тётя крича́ла дя́де: «Он ге́ний!» Дя́дя ра́достно соглаша́лся: «Ещё бы, дорога́я. Настоя́щий ге́ний!» И э́то ведь всё в моём прису́тствии, и у меня́ кружи́лась голова́.

И во́т одна́жды дя́дя меня́ спроси́л:

— А почему́ у тебя́ нет ни одно́й кни́ги твои́х стихов? У Пу́шкина ско́лько их бы́ло… и у Безыме́нского… А у тебя́ ни одно́й…

Действи́тельно, поду́мал я, ни одно́й, но почему́? И э́та печа́льная несправедли́вость так меня́ возбуди́ла, что я отпра́вился в Сою́з писа́телей, на у́лицу Мачабе́ли.

Стоя́ла чудо́вищная тягу́чая жара́, в Сою́зе писа́телей никого́ не́ бы́ло, и лишь оди́н са́мый гла́вный секрета́рь, на моё сча́стье, оказа́лся

It was an unbearably hot day and there wasn't a soul at the Writers' Union office, except, by a happy chance, the Head of the Union. He had dropped in for a moment to pick up some papers, and I arrived just in time to catch him.

"Hello," I said.

"Hello, hello there," he replied, smiling broadly. "Did you want to see me?"

I nodded.

"Well, sit down, please; take a seat. What can I do for you?"

Too naïve to be surprised by either his benevolent smile or his exclamation, I said, "Well, you know, the thing is, I write poems."

"Oooh!" he whispered.

"So, I wanted... I was thinking, why shouldn't I publish a book of poetry... like Pushkin and Bezymensky."

He gazed at me with an inscrutable expression on his face. Now, after all these years, I can perfectly well understand what was behind that expression and what he was certainly thinking, but then...

He stood motionless, with a strange smile on his face. Then he inclined his head a bit and exclaimed, "A book? Of your poems! What a great idea!"

Then he said nothing for a minute; the smile faded and he said sadly: "But you see, we are having problems with... with paper... that's it... we have run out of paper... we don't have any more... we've used up our whole supply."

"Aaah," I sighed, not quite getting his point. "Perhaps my uncle can help out, do you think?"

He walked me to the door.

At home over dinner, I said as if making casual conversation, "I went to the Writers' Union today. They were very glad to see me and said that they would have been delighted to publish my book – but they are having problems with paper... they simply do not have any more."

"Slackers," said my aunt.

"Well, how much paper would they need?" asked my uncle, all business.

в своём кабине́те. Он зае́хал на мину́тку за каки́ми-то бума́гами, и в э́тот моме́нт вошёл я.

— Здра́вствуйте, – сказа́л я.

— О, здра́вствуйте, здра́вствуйте, – широко́ улыба́ясь, сказа́л он. – Вы ко мне?

Я кивну́л.

— О, сади́тесь, пожа́луйста, сади́тесь, я вас слу́шаю!..

Я не удиви́лся ни его́ доброжела́тельной улы́бке, ни его́ восклица́ниям и сказа́л:

— Вы зна́ете, де́ло в том, что я пишу́ стихи́...

— О! – прошепта́л он.

— Мне хо́чется... я поду́мал: а почему́ бы мне не изда́ть сбо́рник стихо́в? Как у Пу́шкина и́ли Безыме́нского...

Он ка́к-то стра́нно посмотре́л на меня́. Тепе́рь, по проше́ствии сто́льких лет, я прекра́сно понима́ю приро́ду э́того взгля́да и о чём он поду́мал, но тогда́...

Он стоя́л не шевеля́сь, и кака́я-то стра́нная улы́бка криви́ла его́ лицо́. Пото́м он слегка́ помота́л голово́й и воскли́кнул:

— Кни́гу?! Ва́шу?!. О, э́то замеча́тельно!.. Э́то бы́ло бы прекра́сно! – Пото́м помолча́л, улы́бка исче́зла, и он сказа́л с гру́стью: – Но, ви́дите ли, у нас тру́дности с э́тим... с бума́гой... э́то самое... у нас ко́нчилась бума́га... её, ну, про́сто нет... фини́та...

— А-а-а, – протяну́л я, не о́чень-то понима́я, – мо́жет быть, я посове́туюсь с дя́дей?

Он проводи́л меня́ до двере́й.

До́ма за обе́дом я сказа́л как бы ме́жду про́чим:

— А я был в Сою́зе писа́телей. Они́ там все о́чень обра́довались и сказа́ли, что бы́ли бы сча́стливы изда́ть мою́ кни́гу... но у них тру́дности с бума́гой... про́сто её нет...

— Безде́льники, – сказа́ла тётя.

— А ско́лько же ну́жно э́той бума́ги? – по-делово́му спроси́л дя́дя.

— Не зна́ю, – сказа́л я, – я э́того не зна́ю.

"I don't know," I answered. "He didn't say."

"Well," he said, "I can come up with a kilogram and a half, maybe two kilograms."

I shrugged my shoulders.

The next day I ran back to the Writers' Union, but no one was there. Even the Head Secretary, lucky for him, was not to be found.

First published in Russian: 1997
Translation by Lydia Stone

– Ну, – сказа́л он, – килогра́мма полтора́ у меня́ найдётся. Ну, мо́жет, два...

Я пожа́л плеча́ми.

На сле́дующий день я побежа́л в Сою́з писа́телей, но там никого́ не бы́ло. И тот, са́мый гла́вный, секрета́рь то́же, на его́ сча́стье, отсу́тствовал.

Munich, 1985

The Power of Art

I am unable to make judgements about my own work or even to comment on it. I can only say that I never make any promises to myself beforehand, nor do I make plans. As for form, I am in favor of tradition. Poems without rhyme and meter, although I understand and respect them, seem foreign to me, amorphous and missing something I find essential. For this reason I continue to learn from the classics or contemporary poets who are true to tradition. I would cite first and foremost, Villon, Pushkin, Kipling (as a poet) and Boris Pasternak.

In danger of succumbing to the bitterness he felt as the result of his war experience, Okudzhava appeared to find salvation in the joy of creation and performance, and his belief in the redeeming power of all fields of art. The first song below, "The Paramount Song," is one of many that not only extolls but demonstrates music's power. This one, however, has an ironic twist that comes in the very last line. Another such poem is the exuberant *"Painters, don't be timid,"* which combines love of Moscow, life and visual art.

The Paramount Song

The best thing that life on Earth brings to me,
That causes most joy in my heart:
I walk, and from nowhere it sings to me,
A song that is longing to start.

Not yet a true song, but developing;
Unripe, like green fruit on the vine.
The melody's splendid, enveloping,
And words fall precisely in line.

From future years it has been sent to me,
Through laughter and tears not yet born,
A trumpeter from the next century
I hear play my song on his horn.

This song puts to music what's best in me –
Original, joyful and light;
This song that I dream is my destiny,
And that I'm unable to write.

1962
Translation by Lydia Stone and Vladimir Kovner

Гла́вная пе́сенка

Наве́рное, са́мую лу́чшую
на э́той земно́й стороне́
хожу́ я и пе́сенку слу́шаю –
она́ шевельну́лась во мне.

Она́ ещё о́чень неспе́тая.
Она́ зелена́ как трава́.
Но чу́дится му́зыка све́тлая,
и стро́го ложа́тся слова́.

Сквозь вре́мя, что мно́ю не про́йдено,
сквозь смех наш коро́ткий и плач
я слы́шу: выво́дит мело́дию
како́й-то гряду́щий труба́ч.

Легко́, необы́чно и ве́село
кру́жит над скреще́ньем доро́г
та са́мая гла́вная пе́сенка,
кото́рую спеть я не смог.

1962

Painters, don't be timid; you must plunge your brushes
In the glow of sunrise and Arbat's melee,
So that all your brushes touch will be as lush as
Leafy forests on the autumn's brightest day.

Painters, you must plunge your brushes in the azure;
Just be true to old traditions and work hard.
Draw all that you see with truth, and love and pleasure,
Like the love we feel on Moscow's boulevards.

Paint our streets awakened, full of animation.
Keep on painting, painters, make the world take heed.
Search for new forms, painters, art needs innovation.
It is not for us to judge if you succeed.

Draw our fates, our summers, autumns, springs and winters
You must judge them, for to you alone they're plain.
Give no thought to us! It's you who were born painters.
All that isn't clear, I promise to explain.

1961
Translation by Lydia Stone and Vladimir Kovner

Живописцы, окуни́те ва́ши ки́сти
в суету́ дворо́в арба́тских и в зарю́,
что́бы бы́ли ва́ши ки́сти сло́вно ли́стья.
Сло́вно ли́стья, сло́вно ли́стья к ноябрю́.

Окуни́те ва́ши ки́сти в голубо́е,
по тради́ции забы́той городско́й,
нарису́йте и приле́жно и с любо́вью,
как с любо́вью мы прохо́дим по Тверско́й.

Мостова́я пусть качнётся, как очнётся!
Пусть начнётся, что ещё не начало́сь!
Вы рису́йте, вы рису́йте, вам зачтётся...
Что гада́ть нам: удало́сь – не удало́сь?

Вы, как су́дьи, нарису́йте на́ши су́дьбы,
на́ше ле́то, на́шу зи́му и весну́...
Ничего́, что мы – чужи́е.
Вы рису́йте! Я пото́м, что непоня́тно, объясню́.

1961

On Tverskoy Boulevard

Bulat Okudzhava

I am driving along Tverskoy Boulevard. With me in the car I have the author's copies of my historical novel, *The Adventures of Shipov*, which I have just received from the publisher. My mood is exultant. The publisher has done a fine job, the book looks good. My book! I continue on my way. Suddenly, something happens. I can't now remember exactly what – something on the road that I have to get around – something unexpected blocking my way. And in front of me is a Traffic Officer, and he orders me to stop. I stop.

He waddles over to the car and salutes me. He's a captain – shortish, chunky, neat, inscrutable, and courteous.

"What were you thinking? Why did you do that?" he says. "Were you in a daze? Please hand over your documents."

I immediately recognize this sort of courtesy. At the very least he is going to accuse me of who knows what, fine me, and chew me out, but he might even confiscate my documents and make my life a misery. Although I no longer remember exactly what happened, I do remember that I was not in any way at fault, and also that I felt quite sure that, nevertheless, he was going to make me suffer. Once he had stopped me, I was not going to get off.

НА ТВЕРСКО́М БУЛЬВА́РЕ

Була́т Окуджа́ва

Еду по Тверско́му бульва́ру. Везу́ в маши́не то́лько что полу́ченные а́вторские экземпля́ры своего́ истори́ческого рома́на «Похожде́ния Шипо́ва». Настрое́ние приподня́тое. Кни́га и́здана прия́тно. Моя́ кни́га. Еду. Вдруг, уже́ сейча́с не по́мню – но что то тако́е на пути́, что то я объезжа́ю, како́е то неожи́данное препя́тствие... А впереди́ – инспе́ктор ГАИ́, и он вели́т мне останови́ться. Остана́вливаюсь.

Он подхо́дит вразва́лочку, берёт под козырёк. Капита́н. Тако́й невысо́кий, пло́тный, аккура́тный, непроница́емый и ве́жливый.

– Что́ же э́то вы? – говори́т он. – Ка́к же э́то так?.. Загляде́лись? Пожа́луйста, ва́ши докуме́нты.

Я хорошо́ зна́ю, что́ за э́той ве́жливостью. Он меня́ отчита́ет неизве́стно за что, оштрафу́ет, поглуми́тся, дай то бог, а ведь мо́жет и докуме́нты отобра́ть, и распя́ть... Сейча́с уже́ не по́мню, что произошло́, по́мню то́лько, что мое́й вины́ не́ было, но по́мню та́кже, что понима́л: всё равно́ нака́жет. Уж е́сли останови́л – не отверте́ться.

"Excuse me, officer," I say, "but there was a trolley right in front of me... and after all I couldn't... and then at the turn... and I was behind a ...

He listens without interrupting and looks in the direction where my shaking hand points. His lips are pressed together and he squints.

"And then," I say, "you can just imagine... "

Suddenly, he speaks.

"You are right. Indeed. I did not consider those points." And he hands me my documents, which he has not even examined.

What just happened? How could this be? A Traffic Officer who acknowledges making a mistake? I am not used to this! I do not know what the proper response is. What should I do now? How can I acknowledge this? Suddenly I remember the copies of my novel! "Oh, officer!"

"Wait a minute!" I say, out of breath, "I simply do not believe that a Traffic Officer has agreed with me. It's a miracle!"

He looks gloomy. He sees my wide smile, but his own lips are tightly pursed.

"You know," I say nervously, "I have just published a historical novel and I would like to present you with a copy."

He looks me over with a slight inclination of his head.

"That's interesting," he says. "Interesting."

"Have a seat in my car, please, and I will sign it for you... "

He settles himself on the seat and takes the book in his hand.

"Interesting," he says. "What is it about?"

"It's about Leo Tolstoy, an actual event in his life."

"Oh, about Tolstoy... I see... And you wrote it?"

"Yes, that's right, I am the author and I want to give you a copy to commemorate our remarkable meeting."

He slams the book shut and holds it out to me.

"Wait just a minute," I say and reach for a pen.

"No," he says, "I have no use for this book."

"What do you mean?" I laugh, not understanding.

– Позвóльте, – говорю́ я, – но ведь там был троллéйбус... А я ведь не дóлжен... и потóм, ведь у поворóта... а я же сзáди...

Он слýшает, не перебивáет меня́. Смóтрит, кудá я покáзываю нéрвной рукóй. Гýбы поджáты, глазá прищýрены.

– И потом, – говорю́ я, – вы тóлько предстáвьте...

И вдруг он говори́т:

– Вы прáвы. Действи́тельно. Этой детáли я не учёл, – и протя́гивает мне докумéнты, в котóрые дáже не заглянýл.

Чтó же это такóе?! Как это так?! Инспéктор ГАИ, признáвший себя́ непрáвым?! Я к этому не привы́к! Я не приспосóблен! Что то нáдо сдéлать... Как то это отмéтить... Тут я вспоминáю, что у меня́ же экземпля́ры ромáна! О, инспéктор!

– Погоди́те, – говорю́ я задыхáясь, – прóсто не вéрится, что инспéктор ГАИ со мной согласи́лся! Чýдо!..

Он хмур, он смóтрит, как я широкó улыбáюсь, но егó гýбы плóтно сжáты.

– Вы знáете, – суетли́во говорю́ я, – у меня́ тóлько что вы́шел истори́ческий ромáн, и я хочý подари́ть вам эту кни́гу.

Он разгля́дывает меня́, чуть наклони́в гóлову.

– Интерéсно, – говори́т он, – интерéсно.

– Прися́дьте, пожáлуйста, в маши́ну, я вам надпишý...

Он устрáивается на сидéнье и берёт в рýки кни́гу.

– Интерéсно, – говори́т он, перели́стывая, – это о чём же?

– Это о Льве Тóлстом, – говорю́ я, – пóдлинное собы́тие в егó жи́зни.

– А, – говори́т он, – о Тóлстом... Да... Это вы написáли?

– Да да, я áвтор, и мне хóчется в знак нáшей удиви́тельной встрéчи подари́ть её вам.

Он захлóпывает кни́гу и протя́гивает её мне.

– Сейчáс, сейчáс, – говорю́ я и тянýсь за рýчкой.

– Да нет, – говори́т он, – эту кни́гу мне не нáдо.

– Тó есть как?! – смеюсь я, ничегó не понимáя.

"Well, you see," he says calmly, "I have already read all about Tolstoy." And he climbs out of the car.

And I watch him walk away, chunky, neat, short-necked, slow. His boots gleam.

First published in Russian: 1997
Translation by Lydia Stone

– А во́т так, – говори́т он споко́йно, – я про Толсто́го все чита́л. – И вылеза́ет из маши́ны.

И я ви́жу, как он ухо́дит – пло́тный, аккура́тный, короткоше́ий, медли́тельный. И сапоги́ его́ блестя́т.

A Great Honor
Bulat Okudzhva

It was the very early sixties. I had already gained some degree of recognition, as tape recorders had come into common use.

The press had begun publishing articles castigating me. This served to increase the public's interest.

It was a tumultuous time for me, and a very significant one. The public had begun to take an interest in me, perhaps not a very broad public, and of course their interest was not so much in me but in my songs, the words of which they repeated to each other, and which they sang, because something in these songs spoke to them.

It was a great honor!

And one day I got a phone call from a man at a hard alloys factory, somewhere near Maria's Grove, on the outskirts of town. He said he was the chairman of the local labor union. There was something strange about his voice; I detected some sort of suspicious undercurrents in his speech. He kept interrogating me. Was I the Okudzhava who sang such and such songs? I said I was indeed. And did I perform them for audiences? Well, yes of course, I did so. "Well in that case, you need to show up at the union club

БОЛЬША́Я ЧЕСТЬ

Була́т Окуджа́ва

Са́мое нача́ло шестидеся́тых. У меня́ уже́ не́которая изве́стность. Кру́тятся магнитофо́ны.

Появля́ются в газе́тах бичу́ющие меня́ фельето́ны. Это ещё бо́льше уси́ливает интере́с ко мне.

Бу́рное для меня́ вре́мя, о́чень значи́тельное. Ведь мно́ю интересу́ется пу́блика, ну, мо́жет быть, и не о́чень широ́кая, ну и, коне́чно, интересу́ются не сто́лько мно́ю, ско́лько мои́ми пе́сенками, кото́рые они́ переска́зывают друг дру́гу, напева́ют, нахо́дят в них что то бли́зкое для себя́...

Больша́я честь.

И во́т однажды звони́т мужчи́на с заво́да твёрдых спла́вов, где то в райо́не Ма́рьиной ро́щи. Называ́ется председа́телем профко́ма. Го́лос у него́ како́й то стра́нный, каки́е то подозри́тельные интона́ции слы́шатся в его́ ре́чи. Он до́лго выспра́шивает меня́ – Окуджа́ва ли я и пою́ ли я свои́ пе́сни... Ах, тот са́мый?.. И выступа́ете с ни́ми?.. Ну да... ну коне́чно... и выступа́ете... Тогда́ вам ну́жно сро́чно к шести́ часа́м быть

at six o'clock on the dot. It is extremely important. You would not believe what a sticky situation has arisen!"

And so I went. The entire way there, I wracked my brain trying to figure out what I could possibly have in common with a hard alloy factory. What the devil were hard alloys, anyway?

There was a crowd at the union club. The all gaped open-mouthed at me, gesturing, exclaiming and cursing.

"Hello, what's all this for?" I asked.

And the union chairman, gasping in agitation, told me what had happened.

It seems that several days earlier, a young man had come to union headquarters: a tall, broad-shouldered young man with a handsome head of flaxen hair and wide, friendly blue eyes.

He was reserved and laconic. He asked if they had ever heard about someone named Okudzhava. They had answered that indeed they had, and what of it? "Well," he had said. "I am Okudzhava, nice to meet you." At this, all the union members rushed over and began to arrange for him to perform at their club. The performance was scheduled for seven o'clock on that very day. This Okudzhava had demanded an advance of 50 rubles, with the rest to be handed over on the day of the performance.

So they gave him the advance, and he left. And a half hour later, the bookkeeper up and told them that it was his impression that Okudzhava looked nothing like this fellow. The famous singer, he believed, was older, shorter, with a mustache... In other words, he sensed something fishy. The union officials started to panic, and after talking to me, they had called in the police. They were expecting him any minute, and were planning to catch him red-handed with me as the witness.

A police lieutenant came up to me and asked for my documents. I gave them to him; they were all in order. He ordered everyone who had no need to be there to leave the premises.

"But the auditorium is packed," someone said.

у нас в профко́ме. Тут де́ло чрезвыча́йной ва́жности... Тут, понима́ете, така́я ка́ша завари́лась!..

Еду. Лома́ю го́лову: что мо́жет быть у меня́ о́бщего с заво́дом твёрдых спла́вов?! Каки́е э́то твёрдые спла́вы?!

В профко́ме мно́жество наро́ду. Все смо́трят на меня́ рази́нув рты, всплёскивают рука́ми, а́хают, чертыха́ются.

— Здра́вствуйте, — говорю́ я, — что э́то случи́лось?

И председа́тель профко́ма, задыха́ясь от волне́ния, расска́зывает мне о происше́дшем.

О том, как не́сколько дней наза́д яви́лся в профко́м молодо́й челове́к высо́кого ро́ста, широкопле́чий. Льняны́е во́лосы украша́ют го́лову. Голубы́е глаза́ дружелю́бно распа́хнуты.

Сде́ржан. Немногосло́вен. Вы про Окуджа́ву что нибудь слыха́ли? Мы говори́м, мол, слыха́ли, слыха́ли, ну и что? А я и е́сть Окуджа́ва, ну, здра́вствуйте. Тут все на́ши сбежа́лись, и мы на́чали сгова́риваться о его́ выступле́нии в на́шем клу́бе. Договори́лись как ра́з на сего́дня, на семь ве́чера. Он сказа́л, что ему́ ну́жен ава́нс в пятьдеся́т рубле́й, а остальны́е, мол, по́сле ве́чера.

Ну, мы да́ли ему́ ава́нс, и он ушёл. И ту́т, че́рез полчаса́, наш бухга́лтер возьми́ и скажи́: по мо́ему, Окуджа́ва во́все не тако́й. Он и по́старше, и поме́льче вро́де, ху́денький тако́й, и у́сики у него́... Что то тут не та́к... Начала́сь у нас па́ника, и во́т сего́дня мы к нача́лу вы́звали опергру́ппу по́сле разгово́ра с ва́ми. Ско́ро он я́вится, представля́ете? И возьму́т его́ с поли́чным, а вы бу́дете свиде́телем!

Ко мне подхо́дит лейтена́нт мили́ции и спра́шивает:

— А докуме́нтики у вас есть?

Предъявля́ю ему́ удостовере́ние. Все в поря́дке. Он говори́т:

— Прошу́ всех ли́шних поки́нуть помеще́ние.

— Пу́блики по́лон зал, — говори́т кто то.

This electrified everyone, me most of all. I started to tremble, especially at the thought of the advance. In those years, 50 rubles was an unheard-of sum for a performance, and this was just the advance! The various clubs where I performed paid at most 30 rubles. And here this impostor had received this huge advance!

It was getting close to eight o'clock, and the crook had still not shown up.

"You won't see hide nor hair of your swindler!" laughed the lieutenant. "He's no fool!"

"Let's wait a little while longer," said the union chairman, although it was clear that he had lost hope.

At eight the chairman said to me, "let's go out on the stage, at least let them get a look at you... What a mess!"

So I stepped up from the wings onto the stage and the audience applauded, and the chairman who had emerged with me, stammering, addressed the hall. "I am sorry to tell you that there has been a misunderstanding. How can I explain it?"

I took the microphone from him and described what had happened. Everyone laughed, applauded and shouted, "Sing! Come on, sing!"

The chairman whispered to me, "Really, maybe you might perform, after all? You see what things have come to... Now we will have to... "

Suddenly, the thought came to me that all this had been planned simply as a way to get me to perform! However, I immediately discarded this idea, because at that time no one had to persuade me to perform, and I considered every invitation to be a great honor. But nevertheless, I shook my head and firmly declined, saying that I was not prepared and had not brought my guitar, so they should clearly understand my position. And so we all went home.

Some years later, during the intermission of one of my performances, someone handed me an envelope containing a photograph of a man I had never seen before. On the back was written: "This man was passing himself off as you at a book fair and autographing your books."

Все наэлектризо́ваны. Я бо́льше всех. Дрожь меня́ сотряса́ет. Осо́бенно когда́ ду́маю о су́мме ава́нса. Ведь в те го́ды пятьдеся́т рубле́й – это была́ неслы́ханная пла́та за выступле́ние, а тут ава́нс! Я, выступа́я по ра́зным клу́бам, получа́л самое бо́льшее трина́дцать рубле́й, а тут ава́нс!

И во́т де́ло уже́ к восьми́, а моше́нника все нет.

– Не придёт ваш жу́лик! – смеётся лейтена́нт. – Что он, дура́к, что ли?

– Подождём ещё немно́го, – говори́т председа́тель профко́ма без вся́кой наде́жды.

В во́семь часо́в председа́тель говори́т мне:

– Пойдёмте, хоть покажи́тесь пу́блике... Вот беда́!

И во́т я выхожу́ из за кули́с на сце́ну, и зал меня́ приве́тствует, и председа́тель, вы́шедший со мной, поте́рянно говори́т в зал:

– Тут, понима́ете, вот какая шту́ка получи́лась... Как бы вам это объясни́ть...

Я отодвига́ю его́ от микрофо́на и расска́зываю о случи́вшемся. Все хохо́чут, аплоди́руют и крича́т:

– По́йте! По́йте!..

Председа́тель ше́пчет мне:

– Мо́жет, вы́ступите?.. Что́ же тепе́рь то... Уж тепе́рь придётся...

Вдруг у меня́ мелька́ет мысль, что все это затея́но специа́льно, чтобы заста́вить меня́ вы́ступить!.. Впро́чем, эта мысль ту́т же га́снет, потому́ что в те го́ды меня́ не ну́жно было угова́ривать и вся́кое приглаше́ние вы́ступить я почита́л за большу́ю честь... И всё таки́ замота́л голово́й и наотре́з отказа́лся, мол, я не гото́вился, и гита́ры со мной нет, и вообще́ вы са́ми ви́дите, как все сложи́лось...

Та́к и разошли́сь.

Че́рез не́сколько лет в переры́ве одного́ из выступле́ний кто то вручи́л мне конве́рт. В нем лежа́ла фотогра́фия незнако́мого мужчи́ны. На оборо́те была́ на́дпись: «Этот челове́к на кни́жной я́рмарке выдава́л себя́ за вас и дава́л авто́графы на ва́ших кни́жках».

Gazing at the photograph, I remembered the long-ago incident at the hard alloys factory. The man in the snapshot was also young, tall and broad-shouldered. But he was a brunet with an impressive mustache in the Ukrainian style.

Nevertheless, it was a great honor!

First published in Russian: 1997
Translation by Lydia Stone

Глядя на э́ту фотогра́фию, я вспо́мнил ту да́внюю исто́рию на заво́де твёрдых спла́вов.

Э́тот то́же был молодо́й челове́к, высо́кий и широкопле́чий. Но он был брюне́т, и у него́ бы́ли пы́шные украи́нские усы́.

И всё таки больша́я честь.

The Private Life of Alexander Pushkin
(or The Nominative Case in Lermontov's Works)
Bulat Okudzhava

An Episode from an Autobiography

It happened a very long time ago. Back then I was young, curly-headed, carefree and successful, and the girls, who are now in their fifties, were recklessly flirting with me. However, the story I want to tell you has nothing to do with those girls, or my first love.

Perhaps like all people in this wonderful period of their life I made mistakes, and many mistakes, but only now do I dare to admit it, as the years have rolled by and the time has come for me to make some confessions. Everything has fallen into place, my ambitions are not what they used to be, my reputation is established. Everybody holds me in the highest esteem now and it is too late, so to say, to worry about my career. In short, as one wise old man liked to say, everybody loves me, and those who hate me I do not want to know. Now at last the time has come to think about my life, re-assess it, break out in a cold sweat and exclaim: "Was that really me?! Did I do all those things?!"

Ча́стная жизнь Алекса́ндра Пу́шкина,
и́ли Имени́тельный паде́ж в тво́рчестве Ле́рмонтова
Була́т Окуджа́ва

Э́то случи́лось о́чень давно́.

Тогда́ я был мо́лод, кудря́в, легкомы́слен и уда́члив, и де́вочки, кото́рым ны́нче за пятьдеся́т, коке́тничали со мной напропалу́ю. Одна́ко исто́рия, о кото́рой я хочу́ рассказа́ть, не име́ет отноше́ния ни к де́вочкам, ни к пе́рвой любви́.

Наве́рное, как все в э́том прекра́сном во́зрасте, я соверша́л оши́бки, и оши́бок бы́ло мно́го, но лишь тепе́рь осме́ливаюсь в них призна́ться, и́бо пролете́ли го́ды и наступи́ло вре́мя и́споведей. Всё вста́ло на свои́ места́, амби́ция уже́ не та, с репута́цией всё утрясло́сь. Тепе́рь все обо́ мне са́мого хоро́шего мне́ния, да́ и о карье́ре, как говори́тся, по́здно уже́ беспоко́иться. Коро́че, как люби́л повторя́ть оди́н дре́вний мудре́ц, все меня́ обожа́ют, а с те́ми, кото́рым я отврати́телен, знако́мств не подде́рживаю. Тепе́рь наконе́ц пришло́ вре́мя вспо́мнить себя́ самого́, оцени́ть, покры́ться холо́дным по́том и воскли́кнуть: «Да я ли э́то был?! Я ли соверша́л всё э́то?!»

When I first arrived in that provincial school everybody gasped: there was a brand-new University badge shining on my breast!

The school was small, unprepossessing, situated in the refectory of a former monastery. The place was remote, far away from any large villages. These were difficult times: the war had ended only some four years earlier. There was a shortage of qualified teachers. Only two of them here had higher education qualifications, and these were only from provincial colleges and obtained on correspondence courses.

And into this kind of school came a man who had graduated from one of the top Universities, a University Arts grad-u-ate, no less!

By the way, I need to tell you something else before I get to the main subject.

When I came back from the frontline and started University, I was accepted without having to take the formal entrance exams, because my military service was taken into consideration. Some understated admiration and "Hurrahs" followed me through the University corridors. Smiles and compliments surrounded me, producing an unjustified confidence in myself. It was enough for me to declare that Gogol was a great Russian writer to produce an ovation in my honor. There was a general opinion that if a young man had fought at the front, it meant that he was almost a humanities expert! I did not go to lectures often: somehow I never had the time. I was not reprimanded. At all of our University gatherings, I would talk about our military campaigns and get credit for it. And the main problem was not that people who were overjoyed because of the victory were too indulgent to one little representative of the victorious army, but that I took it as a credit to myself. And once I had accepted it, it went on like that... But somehow or other I managed to finish my course, somehow wrote my final year course work: something on Mayakovsky. I managed forty pages, got away with bland generalisations. Handing in my work to my tutor, I had the audacity to joke: I am afraid my punctuation leaves something to be desired... Speaking later about my work, my tutor said that the work itself was excellent, only my punctuation left something to be desired. I

Когда́ я появи́лся впервы́е в той се́льской шко́ле, все а́хнули: на груди́ мое́й сверка́л то́лько что возни́кший в приро́де университе́тский значо́к!

Шко́ла была́ ма́ленькая, неказ́истая, в бы́вшей монасты́рской трапе́зной. Ме́сто бы́ло глухо́е, отделённое от кру́пных посёлков. Вре́мя бы́ло тру́дное: го́да четы́ре, как зако́нчилась война́. Дипломи́рованных учителе́й не хвата́ло. Лишь у двои́х бы́ли дипло́мы пединститу́тов, да́ и то перифери́йных, да́ и то зао́чных.

И во́т в э́ту шко́лу, в таку́ю-то шко́лу, прие́хал челове́к, око́нчивший столи́чный университе́т, фи-ло́-ло́г!

Впро́чем, необходи́мо знать ко́е-что́ ещё, пре́жде чем говори́ть о гла́вном.

Когда́ я верну́лся с фро́нта и поступи́л в университе́т, меня́ при́няли без экза́менов. Ти́хое восхищённое «ура́» сопровожда́ло меня́ по университе́тским коридо́рам. Улы́бки и комплиме́нты обвола́кивали меня́ и убаю́кивали. Сто́ило мне, наприме́р, заяви́ть, что Го́голь – вели́кий ру́сский писа́тель, как тотча́с раздава́лись аплодисме́нты в мою́ честь. В во́здухе висе́ло усто́йчивое мне́ние, что е́сли молодо́й челове́к воева́л, зна́чит он – почти́ уже филоло́г. На ле́кции я ходи́л ре́дко: всё бы́ло ка́к-то не́когда. Меня́ не нака́зывали. На всех торже́ственных вечера́х я выступа́л с воспомина́ниями о том, как мы воева́ли, и э́то шло в зачёт. И гла́вная беда́ заключа́лась не в том, что лю́ди, преиспо́лненные ра́дости побе́ды, бы́ли чрезме́рно снисходи́тельны к одному́ ма́ленькому представи́телю победи́вшей а́рмии, а в том, что всё э́то я при́нял на свой ли́чный счёт. А как при́нял, так оно́ и пошло́... Ко́е-как доучи́лся, ко́е-как написа́л дипло́мную рабо́ту: что́-то там тако́е насчёт Маяко́вского, на со́рок страни́ц, натяну́л, отде́лался о́бщими фра́зами. Передава́я рабо́ту своему́ руководи́телю, име́л на́глость пошути́ть: бою́сь, что со зна́ками препина́ния у меня́ не всё в поря́дке... Говоря́ о мое́й рабо́те, он сказа́л, что рабо́та превосхо́дная, то́лько со зна́ками препина́ния не всё в поря́дке. Я по́нял, что он её не чита́л. Меня́ хвали́ли, поздравля́ли, что

understood by this that he had not read it. I was praised, congratulated, it was said that in spite of my war injury, I still got it written, worked hard, made use of a lot of primary and secondary literature (my bibliography was copied from an encyclopaedia). At last, with a University Arts degree and a university badge on my breast, full of, as they say, great expectations, I headed for a small regional town. And I found, to my dismay, that I was the first person in this region with a University education. I was regarded with interest and even reverence.

That was the kind of man that came here!

This man was young, curly-headed, well dressed for those days. He was not so much handsome as attractive, and you could see a great big pair of angel's wings happily flapping on the back of this man from the big city.

The Head of the Regional Educational Department invited his deputy to his office and they started discussing the future of their remarkable guest. The guest thought that he would be asked to head a department in some small pedagogical institute in their decayed little town. But there was not a word about it. He was expecting that he would be offered at least the Headship of the best school in town, but that did not happen either. Instead the Head of the Education Department said that it would be marvellous if the esteemed Arts graduate would go to a faraway village school and work as an ordinary classroom teacher there, enlightening the masses and introducing local teachers to first-rate University scholarship.

At this point I rebelled and declared that my place was really in a town, as I would have to work seriously at my dissertation, which was half-finished and could not be completed without ready access to a town library...

I must say that the idea of the dissertation only came into my head at that moment of impending tragedy. For some reason it had never occurred to me before then. I looked at my interlocuters with some triumph, but they were not abandoning their plans for me that easily. But I – I shouted – was preparing myself for academic research and not for run-of-the-mill school teaching! Do you realise what you are offering me? Yes, we certainly

вот, мол, несмотря на бывшее ранение, всё же написал, поработал, использовал множество литературы (библиографический список я катал из энциклопедии). Наконец с дипломом филолога в кармане и с университетским значком на груди, полный, как это говорится, всяческих радужных надежд, выехал я в небольшой областной город. И оказалось, на мою беду, что в этой области я первый человек с университетским образованием. На меня смотрели с интересом и даже с благоговением.

Вот какой человек приехал в область!

Он был молод, кудряв, по тем временам хорошо одёт. Он был не то чтобы красив, но симпатичен, и два больших счастливых столичных крыла виднелись за его спиной.

Заведующий облоно пригласил своего зама, и они вместе принялись обсуждать судьбу замечательного гостя. Гость предполагал, что ему поручат по меньшей мере заведование кафедрой в маленьком пединституте этого захудалого городка. Но об этом не было ни слова. Он ждал, что ему предложат быть хотя бы директором самой показательной школы города, но и этого не произошло. Вместо всего этого заведующий облоно сказал, что самое замечательное, если уважаемый филолог отправится в далёкую сельскую школу и поработает там учителем, неся свет в массы и приобщая местных учителей к большой университетской науке.

Тут я возмутился и заявил, что лишь в городе моё место, ибо мне... предстоит серьёзная работа над диссертацией, наполовину уже сделанной, которая без городской библиотеки невозможна...

Должен вам сказать, что мысль о диссертации пришла мне в голову именно в этот трагический момент. Раньше я об этом почему-то не думал. Я посмотрел на моих собеседников с торжеством, но они не отказались от своего намерения. Да я, кричал я, готовил себя к научной работе, а не к учительствованию! Вы понимаете, что вы мне

do, they shouted with the deepest respect! We are not sending you to just any old school!..

Me: But I am an Arts grad-u-ate, not some tin pot school teacher!

Them: We are proud of you! Everybody will be proud of you!.. Why would you want a position of a rank and file school teacher in our little town!.. There – you'll be free to do whatever you want.

Me: But I have my dissertation half-finished!

Them: What is the topic of your dissertation?

Me (without hesitation): The nominative case in the works of Lermontov!

Them: Rubbish! Where you will be working, there's even a better topic for your research.

Me: I won't be able to finish my dissertation in your backwaters!

Them: Okay, but Tolstoy used to visit the place where you are going!..

At this point silence fell.

Me (feebly): What on earth did Tolstoy want to go there for?

Them (hurriedly): There is a convent where his sister Maria Nikolayevna used to live. He stayed with her before his death. Do you realise all the research material that is to be had there?.. Solving the mystery of Tolstoy's leaving home is in your hands!

Why not, I thought weakly, it is a possibility... I could write about it... maybe get a story out of it... or even a novel... And this nominative case stuff – it is rubbish really...

To cut a long story short, in about two hours everything was decided, especially when the Head of the Regional Educational Department phoned the Head of the District Educational Department and solemnly declared that a teacher with a University education was coming to their district and he had to be received properly.

You should not forget, he said, – he is the first teacher with a University education in our region!

I took a seat in a small overcrowded bus, bumped along in it for about three hours and eventually came into the district centre. The Head of the District Department did not conceal his happy smile and phoned the Head

предлага́ете? Да мы, крича́ли они́ с благогове́нием, всё понима́ем! Мы ведь не в каку́ю-нибу́дь обыкнове́нную шко́лу вас направля́ем!..

Я: Да я ведь фи-ло-ло́г, а не учители́шка како́й-нибу́дь!

Они́: Мы горди́мся ва́ми! Все ва́ми бу́дут горди́ться! Сдала́сь вам до́лжность рядово́го учи́теля в на́шем городи́шке!.. А там – просто́р.

Я: Но у меня́ диссерта́ция на вы́ходе!

Они́: Кака́я же те́ма ва́шей диссерта́ции?

Я (не коле́блясь): Имени́тельный паде́ж в тво́рчестве Ле́рмонтова!

Они́: Чепуха́! Там, где вы бу́дете рабо́тать, есть те́мка для диссерта́ции ещё почи́ще.

Я: Я не смогу́ зако́нчить диссерта́цию в ва́шей глуши́!

Они́: Зато́ там быва́л Лев То́лстой!..

Тут наступи́ла тишина́.

Я (вя́ло): Что ему́ там пона́добилось?

Они́ (торопли́во): Там в же́нском монастыре́ жила́ его́ сестра́ Мари́я Никола́евна. Он гости́л у неё пе́ред кончи́ной. Вы представля́ете, како́й материа́л?.. Та́йна ухо́да Толсто́го в ва́ших рука́х!

А что, поду́мал я, обесси́лев, мо́жно и впра́вду об э́том... и́ли да́же по́весть... рома́н како́й-нибу́дь... Да́ и э́тот имени́тельный паде́ж – ерунда́ кака́я-то...

Коро́че говоря́, ча́са че́рез два всё сла́дилось, осо́бенно когда́ при мне заве́дующий облоно́ позвони́л заве́дующему районо́ и торже́ственно объяви́л, что к ним в райо́н е́дет учи́тель с университе́тским образова́нием и его́ надлежи́т приня́ть хорошо́, как сле́дует.

– Не забыва́йте, – сказа́л он, – пе́рвый в о́бласти учи́тель с университе́тским дипло́мом!

Я усе́лся в ма́ленький перепо́лненный авто́бусик, потря́сся в нём ча́са три и при́был в райо́нный центр. Заве́дующий районо́, не скрыва́я ра́достной улы́бки, позвони́л дире́ктору шко́лы, распи́сывая меня́ са́мыми фантасти́ческими кра́сками. Зате́м он сам ли́чно проводи́л

teacher of the school, describing me in glowing terms. Then he personally accompanied me to the main road, deposited me on to the back of the passing collective farm lorry and shook my hand...

So there I was, lying on sacks of potatoes and thinking about myself in high-flown terms: so this is how it has all turned out – me, the only teacher with a University diploma in the whole district... Sounds wonderful, doesn't it, there is something in it, great, isn't there; I did the right thing in going to University, and now... good thing I studied in the Humanities Faculty... and now I will collect material on Tolstoy, write a novel about him, and then...

I looked at the other passengers lying next to me and felt sorry for them, as they did not have the slightest idea about the person who was sprawling on the sacks next to them.

And then at last I arrived at the school itself.

Just think, the teacher with the University education, the Arts grad-u-ate!

The teachers were welcoming and respectful to this newcomer. It is true that at first they were somewhat put out as his openness jarred on them. He hid nothing about himself. But eventually they got used to it. And he did not even think of hiding the fact that he had become a teacher by chance. Teaching, he said, was a noble undertaking, of course, but you needed a calling for it, and I was a philologist, I had an academic cast of mind, I needed to finish my dissertation... And I have turned up here by sheer accident, if not by my own stupidity. I got bamboozled by your regional Head. Sochilin or Suchilin – don't remember his name exactly... At this the teachers gasped: how casually he talks about Sochilin himself! How did he get to see him in the first place?.. No problem, he says: just opened the door, came in, sat down, no big deal...

Just think! Sochilin was... God. To get to see the Head of the District Department was quite extraordinary, but look what he did! Just went straight to Sochilin! The only one higher than Sochilin was the Minister of Education himself, and he was an unearthly being, something ethereal, whereas Sochilin was local, regional, albeit still unattainable. The teachers

меня до шоссе́, усади́л в ку́зов случа́йного попу́тного колхо́зного грузовика́ и пожа́л мне ру́ку...

Я лежа́л на мешка́х с карто́шкой и ду́мал о себе́ высокопа́рно: вот, мол, как всё скла́дывается – я еди́нственный в о́бласти учи́тель с университе́тским... Как э́то удиви́тельно звучи́т, что́-то в э́том есть, как э́то всё замеча́тельно; хорошо́, что я поступи́л и́менно в университе́т, и тепе́рь... хорошо́, что я поступи́л на филологи́ческий, и тепе́рь... тепе́рь наберу́ материа́лов о Толсто́м, напишу́ рома́н, и тогда́...

Я гляде́л на случа́йных, похо́жих на меня́ пассажи́ров и жале́л их за то, что они́ не дога́дываются, кто возлежи́т на мешка́х ря́дом с ни́ми.

И во́т наконе́ц при́был я в ту са́мую шко́лу.

Поду́мать то́лько, учи́тель с университе́тским дипло́мом, фи-ло́-лог!

Учителя́ встре́тили его́ дружелю́бно, почти́тельно. Пра́вда, их снача́ла не́сколько коро́било, что он сли́шком уж открове́нно всё о себе́ выкла́дывал, не таи́лся. Но пото́м привы́кли. А он и не ду́мал скрыва́ть, что в учителя́ попа́л случа́йно. Учи́тельствовать, говори́т, коне́чно, благоро́дно, но для э́того ну́жно призва́ние, а я – фило́лог, у меня́ нау́чный склад мышле́ния, мне ну́жно диссерта́цию зака́нчивать... Да́ и попа́л я к вам по стра́нной случа́йности, а мо́жет, да́же по со́бственной глу́пости. Меня́ с то́лку сбил ваш областно́й заве́дующий. Сочи́лин и́ли Сучи́лин – не по́мню... Тут учителя́ а́хнули: как за́просто э́тот о самом Сочи́лине говори́т! Да ка́к э́то так он к нему́ попа́л?.. А во́т та́к и попа́л, говори́т: откры́л дверь, вошёл, сел, поду́маешь...

Ну на́до же! Сочи́лин... бог. К райо́нному за́ву попа́сть – собы́тие, а тут к Сочи́лину взял и вошёл! По́сле Сочи́лина то́лько и есть что мини́стр просвеще́ния, но э́то уже мира́ж, фанта́зия, а Сочи́лин свой,

saw him once every two to three years, and even then in passing, from afar, and this new boy, look at him, just walked in on him!..

But, as the saying goes, all this was only orange blossom, the fruit was yet to come. It did take time to ripen; but time flies – God help you if you don't know that, as I did not know it at the time.

The school year began. The teachers spoke to me in flattering tones: you are a lucky man! Just imagine what knowledge you have. Your methods, too, are probably quite different from ours... Certainly, I said, I was at a University after all. Our education and training were very thorough... You are probably preparing some special plans for your lessons, they said... What are you talking about, I said smiling condescendingly, what plans? What for?.. But how can you do without plans? they exclaimed, how can you do without them? Without plans you'll just have chaos... You are odd, you people, I laughed, do you think that my University knowledge won't be enough for a ninth-grade lesson? Isn't that what I was studying at the University for?.. It is also true that there were teachers who were not impressed by my attitude, and were wispering behind my back: University, University, my word... He's too arrogant, he thinks too much of himself...

Then one day (take note of this!) someone came up to me, I do not remember who it was, and asked me to give a lecture for the collective farmers. I was surprised that people would bother me with such trifles, but the person asking was so respectful that I could not refuse, especially as the lecture was scheduled to be given in a month's time. In a month, I said, it'll be a different matter, as I am now working on my dissertation, and have no time, but in a month I'll be happy to oblige, though I have no idea what I could say to them, and will they understand?... But you could say something simple, he said. They'll listen to you, rest assured. We hardly ever get film shows here, so they are bound to want to listen to you, no doubt about it.

There was a bit of a hiccup when the topic of the lecture was discussed (it turned out that it had to be decided then and there). I had no idea what to lecture on, I had never given any lectures. But I put on a serious

областно́й, недосяга́емый. Учителя́ его́ в два-три го́да раз ви́дели, да́ и то мелько́м, да́ и то издалека́, а э́тот, на́ш-то, взял и вошёл!..

Но всё э́то бы́ли лишь цве́тики, а я́годки мая́чили в отдале́нии. Ещё не наста́л срок им созре́ть, но вре́мя – шту́ка стреми́тельная, упаси́ вас бог не знать э́того, как я не знал когда́-то.

Начали́сь уче́бные дни. Учителя́ говори́ли мне с подобостра́стием: счастли́вчик вы! Э́то ж на́до, каки́е зна́ния, наве́рное. У вас и ме́тоды, наве́рное, совсе́м други́е... Коне́чно, говори́л я, университе́т всё-таки, а не что-нибу́дь. Гото́вили нас основа́тельно... Вы и пла́ны к уро́кам, говори́ли они́, каки́е-нибу́дь осо́бенные составля́ете, наве́рное... Да что́ вы, говори́л я, снисходи́тельно улыба́ясь, каки́е пла́ны?.. Заче́м э́то?.. Как же без пла́нов, а́хали они́, ра́зве без них мо́жно? Да ведь всё перепу́тается... Чудаки́, смея́лся я, да неуже́ли мои́х университе́тских зна́ний не хвата́ет на како́й-то там уро́к в како́м-то девя́том кла́ссе? Сто́ило ли университе́т конча́ть?.. Пра́вда, бы́ли и таки́е учителя́, кото́рые восто́ргов мне не выража́ли, а тихо́нько говори́ли меж собо́й: поду́маешь, университе́т, университе́т... Кичли́в бо́льно, но́сятся тут с ним, са́ми не зна́ют чего́...

И во́т однажды (следи́те внима́тельно) подошёл ко мне кто́-то, сейча́с уже́ и не вспо́мню кто, и предложи́л мне вы́ступить с ле́кцией пе́ред колхо́зниками. Я о́чень удиви́лся, что ко мне подхо́дят с таки́ми пустяка́ми, но тот проси́л так почти́тельно, что отказа́ть бы́ло нельзя́, тем бо́лее что ле́кция намеча́лась че́рез ме́сяц. Че́рез ме́сяц, сказа́л я, друго́е де́ло, а то́ сейча́с я рабо́таю над диссерта́цией, и вре́мени у меня́ нет, а че́рез ме́сяц, пожа́луйста, хотя́ ума́ не приложу́, что́ бы тако́е им рассказа́ть, пойму́т ли... Да вы, сказа́л тот, ка́к-нибудь попро́ще, коне́чно. Слу́шать бу́дут, не сомнева́йтесь. У нас тут кино́ ре́дко быва́ет, та́к что слу́шать бу́дут, не сомнева́йтесь.

Ма́ленький зато́р произошёл при вы́боре те́мы ле́кции (ока́зывается, её ну́жно бы́ло определи́ть и́менно сейча́с). Чёрт её зна́ет, о чём чита́ть, да и не чита́л я никогда́ никаки́х ле́кций. Но лицо́ моё бы́ло

expression, and looked into the distance, screwing up my eyes and rubbing my chin...

It must be said that before my departure into the district, somebody had given me a recently published book, *Pushkin as Recalled by his Contemporaries.* I had dipped into it, reading bits and pieces from time to time. It contained some engaging episodes from Pushkin's life. There was a story, for example, about the young Pushkin having fallen in love with somebody somewhere, and when she rejected him, he ran for nearly 14 *versts* under the scorching sun in a rage! And there were other entertaining stories from the poet's life. And so, suddenly remembering the book, I said that I would probably give a lecture on Pushkin and his life, and the lecture would be called "The Private Life of Alexander Pushkin."

And at that we parted.

Time went by. The weather turned rainy. Then the rains mixed with snow. Then snow started to fall and stayed on the ground. From time to time my eyes fell on that wretched book, *Pushkin as Recalled by his Contemporaries,* and a vague wish to skim its pages took hold of me, but only for a moment. At last, one wonderful day Fate came knocking at my door – respectfully, as it seemed to me – but I did not detect the friendly warning in its knock.

It was a clear, sunny, frosty day, or more precisely, close of day. The sun was setting behind the hill, the very hill where I had to go to bring enlightenment to the masses. Collective farm sledges were standing near my porch. A little horse covered with hoarfrost stood by, impatiently pawing the ground. The coachman was bearded and friendly. I was in a splendid mood. I was a happy-go-lucky hussar. There was no fear, not a care in the world. In their eternal duel between "appearances" and "reality," the former were winning. Oh, my dear University badge, with its combination of white, blue and gold! The love and respect that came with it!

многозначи́тельно, и гляде́л я прищу́рившись в заоко́нные да́ли, и па́льцы мои́ тереби́ли подборо́док...

А на́до сказа́ть, что пе́ред отъе́здом в о́бласть кто́-то подари́л мне то́лько что вы́шедшую кни́гу «Пу́шкин в воспомина́ниях совреме́нников». Я её иногда́ почи́тывал. Там бы́ли любопы́тные исто́рии из жи́зни Пу́шкина. Там, наприме́р, расска́зывалось, как ю́ный Пу́шкин одна́жды где́-то там в кого́-то там влюби́лся и, когда́ им пренебрегли́, в бе́шенстве пробежа́л под паля́щим со́лнцем дли́нный путь, как пото́м оказа́лось – вёрст четы́рнадцать, что́ ли! И ещё там бы́ли вся́кие занима́тельные исто́рии из жи́зни поэ́та. И во́т, вспо́мнив об э́той кни́ге, я сказа́л, что бу́ду чита́ть, пожа́луй, ле́кцию о Пу́шкине, о его́ жи́зни, и называ́ться ле́кция бу́дет: «Ча́стная жизнь Алекса́ндра Пу́шкина».

На том и расста́лись.

Шло вре́мя. Начали́сь дожди́. Пото́м дожди́ перемеша́лись со сне́гом. Пото́м вы́пал снег и уже́ бо́льше не раста́ял. Иногда́ на глаза́ мне попада́лась э́та прокля́тая кни́га «Пу́шкин в воспомина́ниях совреме́нников», и ту́склое, едва́ улови́мое жела́ние перелиста́ть её страни́цы овладева́ло мной, но лишь на одно́ мгнове́ние. Наконе́ц в оди́н прекра́сный день рука́ мое́й форту́ны почти́тельно, как мне показа́лось, постуча́ла в мою́ дверь, и я не смог улови́ть в том сту́ке дру́жеского предостереже́ния.

Был я́сный со́лнечный моро́зный день, верне́е – исхо́д дня. Со́лнце клони́лось за приго́рок, за тот са́мый, куда́ мне предстоя́ло е́хать, чтобы нести́ свет в ма́ссы. У крыльца́ стоя́ли колхо́зные са́ни. Заиндеве́вшая лоша́дка перебира́ла нога́ми. Возни́ца был борода́т и приве́тлив. Настрое́ние у меня́ бы́ло превосхо́дное. Я каза́лся себе́ счастли́вым гуса́ром. Не́ было ни стра́ха, ни да́же волне́ния. В изве́чном поеди́нке меж «слыть» и «быть» верх одерживало пе́рвое. О мой дорого́й университе́тский значо́к, соедине́ние бе́лого, си́него и золото́го! Как я люби́м и почита́ем!

The horse was running briskly. I felt no fear. The remarkable book was resting on my knees, a weighty tome – the source of inspiration for a young scholar, a treasure trove of success and fame... I felt no fear.

The Collective farm hall was situated in a spacious, old log house. After six kilometers of frosty road, it was pleasant to go into the warmth and to sense those respectful looks on me. I felt no fear. My audience was sitting on the benches. There were old people and children. There were many young people. Some were sitting in pairs. On a simple stage there stood a long table, covered with faded red cloth. Kerosene lamps were burning. There was a raised platform, a sort of "lectern" standing to the right of the table. Everything was as it should be. The collective farm chairman was sitting alone at the table. Oh, my dear University... I felt no fear.

Well, said the chairman as I nonchalantly mounted the stage, and now our dear teacher will tell us about the private life of Alexander Sergeyevich Pushkin. Let's listen carefully. And, turning to me: Will an hour and a half be enough?

Who knows? I said with a smile, I will do my best in any case.

Oh, no, he said, we have plenty of time: talk as long as you like, I am just asking...

Well, perhaps I might take half an hour extra, I said jokingly. Don't blame me...

Everybody was smiling. Contact with the audience was established.

I took my place in the lectern. I put my watch in front of me on one side, and on the other – that wonderful book with the fascinating title, *Pushkin as Recalled by his Contemporaries*. I felt no fear.

Pushkin – is a great Russian poet! I exclaimed in a bright, inspired and passionate tone.

Everybody agreed with me. They were looking straight at me, as if from a family photo. Oh, my dear Univer...

Why am I trembling? I thought.

To this very day I recall that moment with horror: fear seized me, a fear that I had not experienced even on the frontline during the war. What else

Лоша́дка бежа́ла ре́зво. Стра́ха не́ было. Замеча́тельная кни́га покоилась на моих коле́нях, тяжёленькая, пло́тненькая такая – исто́чник вдохнове́ния молодо́го учёного, кладова́я успе́ха, сла́вы... Стра́ха не́ было.

В большо́й ста́рой бреве́нчатой избе́ размеща́лся колхо́зный клуб. По́сле шестикилометро́вого моро́зного пути́ бы́ло прия́тно войти́ в тепло́ и ощути́ть на себе́ почти́тельные взо́ры. Стра́ха не́ было. На ла́вках сиде́ли мои́ слу́шатели. Бы́ли старики́ и де́ти. Бы́ло мно́го молоды́х люде́й. Не́которые сиде́ли па́рами. На нехи́трой сце́не стоя́л дли́нный стол, покры́тый кра́сной вы́цветшей мате́рией. Сия́ли кероси́новые ла́мпы. Спра́ва от стола́ возвыша́лось подо́бие ка́федры. Всё как полага́ется. За столо́м в одино́честве сиде́л председа́тель колхо́за. О мой дорого́й университе́тский... Стра́ха не́ было.

– Ну во́т, – сказа́л председа́тель, когда́ я легко́ взлете́л на подмо́стки, – сейча́с наш дорого́й учи́тель расска́жет нам о ча́стной жи́зни Алекса́ндра Серге́евича Пу́шкина. Послу́шаем внима́тельно. – И, оборотившись ко мне: – Ча́сика в полтора́ уло́житесь?

– Кто его́ зна́ет, – улыбну́лся я, – во вся́ком слу́чае, бу́ду стара́ться.

– Да нет, – сказа́л он, – вре́мя у нас есть: ско́лько ну́жно, сто́лько и расска́зывайте, э́то я так...

– Ну, мо́жет, с полча́сика ли́шнего прихвачу́, – пошути́л я. – Не взыщи́те...

Все заулыба́лись. Конта́кт был.

Я встал за ка́федру. С одно́й стороны́ положи́л пе́ред собо́й свои́ часы́, с друго́й стороны́ – замеча́тельную кни́гу с завора́живающим загла́вием «Пу́шкин в воспомина́ниях совреме́нников». Стра́ха не́ было.

– Пу́шкин – вели́кий ру́сский поэ́т! – воскли́кнул я легко́, вдохнове́нно и стра́стно.

Все со мной бы́ли согла́сны. Гляде́ли на меня́, не отводя́ глаз, как с семе́йной фотогра́фии. О мой дорого́й униве́р...

«Отчего́ э́то я трясу́сь?» – поду́мал я.

Я с у́жасом да́же сейча́с вспомина́ю э́ту мину́ту: страх охвати́л меня́, страх, кото́рого я не испы́тывал да́же на фро́нте: о чём говори́ть да́льше?

should I say? How should I make the whole thing hang together? If only I had a little tiny scrap of scruffy, cramped paper and if only on it there were some scarcely legible lines in bad handwriting, about what I had read in that wretched book! But in front of me there was only the sloping, scruffy desk of a fine lectern, and on it lay a silent book, heavy as a mill-stone round my neck. I looked at my watch – a minute and a half had passed...

As my presence of mind was slipping away I remembered our very best University professor. How easily he used to deliver his lectures! How he conducted himself, utterly at ease! His erudition was enough for ten lecturers at least. He seemed unaware of his audience, his words used to pour out easily, like verse.

I looked at my watch again – a minute and a half had passed.

Once, I said, holding the desk tightly, the young Pushkin... fell in love somewhere in the south... with a gypsy... She was indifferent to him, and he, in anger, ran twenty-four kilometers in terrible heat... – they were listening to me with attention – not meters but kilometers...

Silence reigned. I remembered another University lecturer. He used to walk to and fro in front of us as he spoke. Sometimes he gave the impression that he had a walking stick in his hand and a chrysanthemum in his button-hole.

Twenty-four kilometers! I exclaimed. Can you imagine it?

The people in the hall were silent. I looked at my watch – two minutes had passed.

Somebody cleared his throat... Oh, if only he had coughed properly and at length! There is a kind of cough when the whole body is wracked, the face goes dark red, and the sound is like thunder. Or if only he would start talking to his neighbor and would say loudly something like: "Vas', hey Vas', what is he doing there? Let's go home... " At that point I would say sarcastically: "Okay, I know it's a waste of time, listening to someone banging on about Pushkin, it is much better to go home and lie down somewhere warm by the stove." Or something like that. But there was silence in the house... And it was also possible to have a drunk in the audience. He could have dropped

Как увязать то, что следует увязать? Если бы передо мной лежал хотя бы маленький, ничтожный клочок измятой линованной бумаги и если бы на нём пусть вкривь и вкось, нелепым почерком, неразборчиво было бы написано, набросано, едва угадывалось бы то, что я вычитал когда-то из этой проклятой книги! Но передо мной была наклонная потёртая доска замечательной кафедры и на ней лежала молчаливая книга, тяжёлая, словно камень на шее. Я посмотрел на часы – прошло полторы минуты...

Теряя сознание, я вспомнил самого лучшего нашего университетского профессора. Как легко он читал свои лекции! Как свободно держался! Его эрудиции хватило бы на десятерых лекторов. Он не замечал аудитории, слова лились как стихи.

Я снова посмотрел на часы – прошло полторы минуты.

– Однажды, – сказал я, крепко держась рукой за кафедру, – молодой Пушкин... где-то на юге влюбился... кажется, в цыганку... Она была к нему равнодушна, и он, разозлившись, пробежал по жаре двадцать четыре километра... – слушали меня внимательно, – не метра, а километра...

Стояла тишина. Я вспомнил другого преподавателя университета. Читая лекции, он вальяжно прогуливался перед нами. Иногда даже казалось, что в руке у него – трость, а в петличке – хризантема.

– Двадцать четыре километра! – выкрикнул я. – Представляете?..

Собравшиеся молчали. Я посмотрел на часы – прошло две минуты. Кто-то робко кашлянул... О, если бы он раскашлялся как следует и надолго! Бывает же такая форма кашля, когда всё тело сотрясается, лицо багровеет и грохот стоит необычайный. Или, например, начал бы переговариваться с соседом, сказал бы, например, громко: «Вась, а Вась, чего это он там? Пошли домой... » Тут бы я сказал с насмешкой: «Конечно, слушать о Пушкине – пустая трата времени, лучше завалиться на печь... » Или что-нибудь в этом роде. Но в клубе стояла тишина... А ведь мог здесь оказаться кто-нибудь и выпивший. Взял бы и запел... Тут бы я развёл руками

in by chance... If that had been the case, I could have spread my hands in a gesture of helplessness and said to the chairman: "Well, you know, under these circumstances there's no point in giving a lecture about a great poet – you'd be better off operating a threshing machine. I've come six kilometers in freezing cold weather. Do you think I need this? I tore myself away from work on my dissertation..." And I would storm off the stage and make for the exit!

But there was silence in the club.

Or, for example, there was another episode, I said, and my own voice seemed strange to me... *What episode? What episode?* – boomed in my head. The damned wonderful book lay before me and my pale trembling fingers clutched it as if this was my last hope. How could I, such an idiot, forget about it! I will now look into it, flick through it, and quickly find... *What episode? What episode?...* Or, for example, such an episode, I slowly repeated. It is well known... *What is well known? What is known?...* Suddenly I came across the name of Natalya Goncharova. It came to me in a flash. Pushkin was married to Natalya Goncharova! I exclaimed. She was a beauty. Just before his marriage he met a gypsy girl called Tanya... no, Stesha... And here they... *What about them? What about them?...* I looked at my watch – four minutes had passed.

Something has happened to my watch, I said to the chairman. He took off his watch hurriedly and gave it to me. I put it next to mine. Both showed the same time. *Calm down*, I said to myself. *Now I should start striding up and down the stage as I talk* – but I could not tear my hands from the pulpit.

Just a minute, I said. My bookmark has fallen out of my book, and therefore... now... so... This is a remarkable book... so, you see... in such a way...

The pages were turning over by themselves, in the order known only to themselves: Danzas, Vyazemsky, autumn in Boldino, the tsar... The tsar!

Aha, I said with relief. You certainly all know that the tsar did not like Pushkin... But you probably do not know, probably do not know... *What don't they know, what don't they know?...* The tsar sent him into exile to the village of Mikhailovskoe... no, first of all he exiled him to Odessa, where

и сказа́л председа́телю: «Ну, зна́ете, в тако́й обстано́вке не ле́кцию о вели́ком поэ́те чита́ть, а молоти́лку крути́ть. Я шесть киломе́тров е́хал сюда́ по моро́зу! Вы ду́маете, э́то мне ну́жно? От диссерта́ции вре́мя оторва́л... » И бы́стро-бы́стро сошёл бы со сце́ны – и в две́ри!

Но в клу́бе стоя́ла тишина́.

– И́ли, наприме́р, тако́й слу́чай, – сказа́л я не свои́м го́лосом... «Како́й слу́чай? Како́й слу́чай?» – загуде́ло в голове́. Прокля́тая замеча́тельная кни́га лежа́ла пе́редо мной, и мои́ бле́дные трясу́щиеся па́льцы впили́сь в неё с после́дней наде́ждой. Как мог я, идио́т, позабы́ть о ней! Сейча́с я загляну́ в неё, посмотрю́ туда́, бы́стренько перелиста́ю, найду́... «Како́й слу́чай? Како́й слу́чай?..»

– И́ли, наприме́р, тако́й слу́чай, – ме́дленно повтори́л я. – Хорошо́ изве́стно... – «Что хорошо́ изве́стно? Что изве́стно?..» Внеза́пно я наткну́лся на и́мя Ната́льи Гончаро́вой. Вспы́хнул ослепи́тельный свет. – Пу́шкин был жена́т на Ната́лье Гончаро́вой! – воскли́кнул я. – Она́ была́ краса́вица. Перед самой жени́тьбой он встре́тился с цыга́нкой Та́ней... нет, Сте́шей... И тут они́... – «Что они́? Что они́?..»

Я посмотре́л на часы́ – прошло́ четы́ре мину́ты.

– Что́-то с мои́ми часа́ми, – сказа́л я председа́телю.

Он торопли́во снял свои́ и пода́л их мне. Я положи́л их ря́дом со свои́ми. И те, и други́е пока́зывали одина́ковое вре́мя. «Споко́йно, – сказа́л я сам себе́. – Сейча́с ну́жно расска́зывать, проха́живаясь по сце́не», – но рук от ка́федры оторва́ть не смог.

– Одну́ мину́точку, – сказа́л я, – тут из кни́жки вы́пала закла́дка, и потому́... вот сейча́с... зна́чит, так... Это замеча́тельная кни́га... зна́чит, так... . таки́м о́бразом...

Страни́цы перели́стывались са́ми, в како́м-то им одни́м изве́стном поря́дке: Данза́с, Вязе́мский, о́сень в Болдине́, царь... Царь!

– Ага́, – сказа́л я с облегче́нием. – Вы, коне́чно, все зна́ете, что царь Пу́шкина не люби́л... Но вы, наве́рное, не зна́ете, наве́рное, не зна́ете... – «Чего́ не зна́ете? Чего́ не зна́ете?..» – Он сосла́л его́ в село́ Миха́йловское... нет, снача́ла он сосла́л его́ в Оде́ссу, где губерна́тором

the governor was Count Vorontsov. Vorontsov did not like Pushkin and sent him out to look for locusts. When locusts gather in great numbers… when locusts gather in great numbers…

I tried to take off my University badge on the quiet but could not; I wanted to turn the page of the book, but the book did not open at all. I looked at my watch – seven minutes had passed. The chairman's watch showed the same time.

I should have prepared a plan, was the thought that dawned on me in the middle of this madness, and I should have found examples to illustrate every point in the plan. Then I could have read the whole thing straight through without stopping. The chairman would then come up to me to remind me that the time was up, and somebody from the audience would shout: "Let him go on!"

I looked at the chairman. He looked pensive and all the others did too. Maybe they were thinking about Count Vorontsov at that moment, or perhaps about Natalya. In all probability none of them was thinking about me and nobody suspected how I was dreaming that the floor under my feet might open wide, that flames might envelope the log cabin, that somebody would shout "Wolves!" – and everybody would rush to the windows, and I would say: "Well, you know, under these circumstances… "

Would anybody have any questions? I asked the chairman as calmly as I could.

Have you finished? he asked without any surprise.

Yes, that's probably it, I said, not hearing my own voice.

Then the chairman got up and asked:

Are there any questions?

There were no questions.

I wish they had rushed onto the stage and killed me! I thought.

Well then, said the chairman, if there are no questions, let's kill him!..

Actually, that was what I thought, but he said:

Well, if there are no questions, let's thank our teacher – and he started applauding. He received some unenthusiastic support. And this young,

был граф Воронцо́в. Воронцо́в Пу́шкина не люби́л и посла́л его́ на саранчу́... Когда́ саранча́ собира́ется в большо́м коли́честве... когда́ саранча́ собира́ется в большо́м коли́честве...

Я попыта́лся незаме́тно отвинти́ть университе́тский значо́к, но не смог, хоте́л переверну́ть страни́цу кни́ги, но кни́га не открыва́лась вообще́. Я посмотре́л на свои́ часы́ – прошло́ семь мину́т. На часа́х председа́теля было то́ же са́мое.

«Ну́жно было соста́вить план, – осени́ло меня́ в э́том безу́мии, – и к ка́ждому пу́нкту пла́на подыска́ть приме́ры. Я бы чита́л и чита́л без остано́вки. Подошёл бы ко мне председа́тель, что́бы напо́мнить, что вре́мя вы́шло, а из за́ла кри́кнули бы: «Пусть чита́ет!»

Я посмотре́л на председа́теля. Он был заду́мчив, и всё остальны́е то́же. Мо́жет быть, они́ ду́мали в э́тот моме́нт о гра́фе Воронцо́ве, а мо́жет быть, о Ната́лье. Наве́рное, никто́ не ду́мал обо́ мне, никто́ не подозрева́л, как я мечта́л, что́бы пол под мои́ми нога́ми развёрзся, что́бы пла́мя охвати́ло бреве́нчатый клуб, что́бы кто-нибу́дь кри́кнул: «Во́лки!» – и всё бро́сились бы к о́кнам, а я сказа́л бы: «Ну, зна́ете, в тако́й обстано́вке... »

– Мо́жет быть, бу́дут каки́е-нибудь вопро́сы? – спроси́л я у председа́теля как мог споко́йно.

– Вы уже́ зако́нчили? – спроси́л он без те́ни удивле́ния.

– Да, пожа́луй, и всё, – сказа́л я, не слы́ша со́бственного го́лоса.

Тогда́ председа́тель встал и спроси́л:

– Каки́е бу́дут вопро́сы? Но вопро́сов не было.

«Хоть бы они́ бро́сились на сце́ну и уби́ли меня́!» – поду́мал я.

– Ну что ж, – сказа́л председа́тель, – раз нет вопро́сов, дава́йте его́ убьём!..

Впро́чем, э́то я так поду́мал, а он сказа́л:

– Ну что же, е́сли нет вопро́сов, дава́йте поблагодари́м това́рища учи́теля, – и зааплоди́ровал. Его́ вя́ло поддержа́ли. А э́тот молодо́й, кудря́вый, уда́чливый, с новёхоньким университе́тским значко́м

curly-headed, happy-go-lucky chap with his brand new University badge on his breast looked round the hall hurriedly, like a rabbit, and his young lips trembled, and his fingers did not obey him.

Nobody noticed how he found himself outside. A six kilometers return trip awaited through ravines and copses. It was dark. It was windy and the snow was falling. And he imagined himself crawling towards the log house, covered with blood... He walked slowly, unsteadily. Suddenly there was the sound of a sledge runner, and the same collective farm sledge caught up with him.

They told me to get you home, said the bearded coachman merrily. Take a seat, teacher. You were in too much of a hurry to leave...

I sat down in the sledge and started crying.

... Many years have passed since that time. In those days I was young, curly-headed and successful, and, taking off my badge, I threw the wretched blue, white and gold thing into the snow. It is possible that in a hundred years' time some academic researchers will find it and start speculating about the fate of its owner...

March 1976
Translation by Natalia Gogolitsyna

на груди́ огляде́л зал торопли́во, по-за́ячьи, и его́ молоды́е гу́бы дрожа́ли, и па́льцы не слу́шались.

Как он очути́лся на у́лице, никто́ не успе́л заме́тить. Шестикилометро́вый обра́тный путь лежа́л че́рез овра́ги и переле́ски. Бы́ло темно́. Вью́жило. И он предста́вил, как, окрова́вленный, подполза́ет к клу́бу... Он шёл ме́дленно, его́ пока́чивало. Внеза́пно послы́шался скрип поло́зьев, и те са́мые колхо́зные са́ни догна́ли меня́.

— Ве́лено домо́й доста́вить, — ве́село сказа́л борода́тый возни́ца, — сади́сь, учи́тель. Бо́льно ты на но́гу скор...

Я усе́лся в са́ни и запла́кал.

... С тех по́р прошло́ мно́го лет. Тогда́ я был мо́лод, кудря́в и уда́члив, и, отвинти́в, я бро́сил в снег своё ромбови́дное несча́стье, си́нее, бе́лое и золото́е. Быть мо́жет, лет че́рез сто учёные его́ обнару́жат и бу́дут до́лго гада́ть о судьбе́ владе́льца...

Март, 1976

The Freedom of the Artist

... If the intonation (of a song) expressing the poet's individuality is there, if an individual's fate is felt behind the song, only then will it be a work of art.

** * **

It is ridiculous to value popularity. And, after all, as the poet Nikola Dorizo said:

> *Popularity is laughable and unfaithful*
> *That's how she was created*
> *Fame is the only faithful lady*
> *But she is not a wife but a widow.*

For this reason, it makes no sense to concern oneself with popularity. On the other hand, independence is a very fine thing.

** * **

I long to see human beings feel themselves to be the full creators of their own lives. This is why the great Russian literature of the nineteenth century, which upholds individual and human freedom, is so dear to me.

In his writings about art, Okudzhava makes it very clear how important he considers the independence, individuality and freedom of the artist if the latter is to fulfill his all-important role. The first poem in this section, "Guitar," describes what is essentially Okudzhava's own experience as a still-struggling bard, trying to fulfill his artistic destiny one small concert venue at a time. In the poem's touching and bittersweet ending, instead of self-pity the poet expresses sympathy for his instrument. In the second poem, "Song about Mozart," Okudzhava makes atypically strong political statements, possibly because the subject is set so far back in the past. The poet exhorts Mozart, and by implication all artists, to ignore personal criticism and to concentrate on their art for the sake of humanity.

In "That Lucky Pushkin," Okudzhava in the style of comic verse lists all the reasons that Pushkin might be considered lucky, including the surprising benefits of the government actions that curtailed his freedom and independence throughout his life – for example, the police who were in charge of monitoring him in exile were fans of his poetry. The real irony here is that from the standpoint of freedom of expression, freedom of movement and ability to get published and read, Pushkin – even in exile – truly was a great deal more fortunate than most talented Soviet poets, and many hearing this song would be well aware of that fact.

Guitar

I am so weary; my feet are dragging,
Guitar dislodging with every step.
But hope's persistent – it keeps on nagging.
September rain: we are soaking wet.

We've been performing; I've gotten used to
The rain, the wind, to the rain and you.
Well, let them rant, those who would refuse to
Admit our age has a place for you.

Let them disparage us to our faces,
From envy scorn us, if they so please.
I trudge on in my guitar's embraces
As, in her wisdom, she holds her peace.

You're not the first on whom our ungrateful
And bitter century has heaped disdain.
Oh my guitar, you who've been so faithful!
Let me at least clear your cheeks of rain.

1961
Translation by Lydia Stone and Vladimir Kovner

Гита́ра

Уста́лость но́ги едва́ воло́чит,
Гита́ра ко́рчится под руко́й.
Наде́жда го́лову мне моро́чит,
А дождь сентя́брьский льёт тако́й.

Мы из компа́нии. Мне привы́чны
И дождь и ве́тер, и дождь и ты.
Пуска́й болта́ют, что не типи́чны
В двадца́том ве́ке твои́ черты́.

Пусть друг недо́лгий в нас ка́мень ки́нет,
Пуска́й зави́стник своё кричи́т-
Моя́ гита́ра меня́ обни́мет,
Интеллиге́нтно она́ смолчи́т.

Тебе́ не пе́рвой, тебе́ не пе́рвой
Предъя́влен ве́ком суро́вый счёт.
Моя́ гита́ра, мой спу́тник ве́рный,
Дава́й хоть дождь смахну́ со щёк.

1961

Song about Mozart

Mozart is fiddling, in joy, exaltation.
Mozart's old fiddle sings song after song.
Mozart belongs to the world, not one nation.
Mozart keeps fiddling his whole short life long.

Artists live lives not without dissipation.
That doesn't matter, as all artists know.
Maestro, keep fiddling, maintain concentration.
Maestro, keep fiddling, don't put down your bow.

Yet in the end, we will find that we're grateful
Even for this life fate gave us to live.
Let us not make of our fatherland fateful
An idol whose sins we yet cannot forgive.

Artists live lives not without dissipation.
That doesn't matter, as all artists know.
Maestro, keep hoping, hope yields inspiration.
Maestro, keep fiddling, don't put down your bow.

Youth is as brief, bright and hot as a fire;
Flame turns to smoke and we see it no more.
Music will last, but all else will expire,
Fade like the once flame-red coat Mozart wore.

Artists live lives not without dissipation.
That doesn't matter, as all artists know.
Maestro, ignore all that hinders creation.
Maestro, keep fiddling, don't put down your bow.

1969
Translation by Lydia Stone and Vladimir Kovner

Пе́сенка о Мо́царте

Мо́царт на ста́ренькой скри́пке игра́ет,
Мо́царт игра́ет, а скри́пка поёт,
Мо́царт оте́чества не выбира́ет —
про́сто игра́ет всю жи́знь напролёт.

Ах, ничего́, что всегда́, как изве́стно,
на́ша судьба́ — то гульба́, то пальба́...
Не оставля́йте стара́ний, маэ́стро,
не убира́йте ладо́ни со лба.

Где́-нибу́дь на остано́вке коне́чной
ска́жем спаси́бо и э́той судьбе́.
Но из грехо́в свое́й ро́дины ве́чной
не сотвори́ть бы куми́ра себе́.

Ах, ничего́, что всегда́, как изве́стно,
на́ша судьба́ — то гульба́, то пальба́...
Не расстава́йтесь с наде́ждой, маэ́стро,
не убира́йте ладо́ни со лба.

Ко́ротки на́ши лета́ молоды́е.
Миг — и разве́ются, как на костра́х,
кра́сный камзо́л, башмаки́ золоты́е,
бе́лый пари́к, рукава́ в кружева́х.

Ах, ничего́, что всегда́, как изве́стно,
на́ша судьба́ — то гульба́, то пальба́...
Не обраща́йте внима́нья, маэ́стро,
не убира́йте ладо́ни со лба.

1969

That Lucky Pushkin

Our Pushkin's luck can't be denied!
His life was splendid!
In exile in the countryside,
his heartache mended.

The mill wheels hummed the livelong day,
with skylarks soaring.
A fair was not too far away
if life got boring.

His craft was of the highest sort;
his pen – a rapier;
His wit so quick that verse was sport
with words and paper.

In Black Sea towns he made a splash;
in style he'd ride!
And people always loaned him cash
until he died.

When he was exiled to a place
(such were the times),
the gendarmes who were on his case
all knew his rhymes.

To chat with him the tsar was pleased
and even showed it.
Who'd not be glad to shoot the breeze
With such a poet?

He'd worshipped beauty, he confessed,
unchastely, but with vigor.
And famed for beauty was Dantes
who pulled his final trigger.

A principle worth dying for –
The honor he defended.
And there upon the river shore
His short life ended.

1967

Translation by Lydia Stone and Vladimir Kovner

Счастли́вчик Пу́шкин

Алекса́ндру Серге́ичу хорошо́!
Ему́ прекра́сно!
Гуди́т ме́льничное колесо́,
боль уга́сла,

ба́ба щу́рится из избы́,
в небе – жа́воронки,
то́лько де́сять мину́т езды́
до бли́жней я́рмарки.

У него́ ремесло́ пе́рвый сорт
и перо́ о́стро.
Он губа́ст и уче́н как че́рт,
и всё ему́ про́сто:

жил в Оде́ссе, быва́л в Крыму́,
е́здил в каре́те,
де́ньги в долг дава́ли ему́
до са́мой сме́рти.

О́чень ве́жливы и тихи́,
дела́ми заму́ченные,
жанда́рмы его́ стихи́
на па́мять зау́чивали!

Да́же царь приглаша́л его́ в дом,
жела́я при э́том
потрепа́ться о том о сем
с таки́м поэ́том.

Он краси́вых же́нщин люби́л
любо́вью не чи́нной,
и да́же уби́т он был
краси́вым мужчи́ной.

Он уме́л бума́гу мара́ть
под треск све́чки!
Ему́ бы́ло за что умира́ть
у Чёрной ре́чки.

1967

Irony and its Allies

Sadness and irony (are) the characteristics of my maturity as a writer.

** * **

I... include among the poets I feel closest to, the Pole Julian Tuwim.[1] *Tuwim perceives life sadly and ironically, as do I. Actually, this feeling is characteristic of all poets who are more sensitive than others, and who, despite it being painful, are aware of how imperfect the world is. A completely serious viewpoint has always seemed somewhat suspect to me, and a competely cheerful viewpoint sends me into a panic.*

The *American Heritage Dictionary* defines irony as "the use of words to express something different and often opposite to their literal meaning; a deliberate contrast between apparent and intended meaning of what is said." In societies marked by censorship and repercussions for dissent,

---

1. Julian Tuwim (1894-1953) was a Polish poet of Jewish origin and a leading figure of 20th century Polish literature. After founding the experimental *Skamander* group in 1919, Tuwim became known for his satirical poetry and children's rhymes. His translations of Pushkin and other Russian poets into Polish were widely admired.

irony becomes a key weapon in the arsenal of dissenting writers, a seemingly innocent way of calling attention to the ills of society.

This is certainly the case with Bulat Okudzhava. Even in one of his earliest poems, "*The ranks of real humans have dwindled,*" his mastery of this tone is impressive. In "*A brash new Muse I have invented,*" he names irony outright as his own particular Muse. This is a rather late poem, and a comment on decades of previous work.

"Prayer," sometimes referred to as "Francois Villon's Prayer," is one of the most famous of Okudzhava's poems. In it, the irony of the contrast between what humans have and what they need pertains not so much to a particular society, but to all of God's world. In the final poem, and the most amusing one included in this issue, Okudzhava gently satirizes the pettiness and futility of war by setting it in a fairy (or folk) tale world.

The ranks of real humans have dwindled.
You who say "now's their era" are blind.
Try to count, (but take care you're not swindled),
In each district, how many you find.

For such beings our need is profound,
But on Earth a scant handful are known.
In our land, just my Mama's been found.
Tell me, what can she do on her own?

1956
Translation by Lydia Stone and Vladimir Kovner

A brash new Muse I have invented,
Ironic, for our Earth severe.
To her I've vast domains presented
Bade her play pranks, and smirk and sneer.

Old Zeus's nine fair haughty daughters,
Who hold themselves in such esteem,
Just can't achieve a thing without her,
No matter how they squirm and scheme.

1985
Translation by Lydia Stone

Настоя́щих люде́й так немно́го,
Все вы врёте, что век их наста́л.
Посчита́йте и че́стно и стро́го,
Ско́лько бу́дет на ка́ждый кварта́л.

Настоя́щих люде́й о́чень ма́ло.
На плане́ту – совсе́м ерунда́.
А на Росси́ю одна́ моя́ ма́ма.
То́лько что она́ мо́жет одна́?

1956

Я вы́думал му́зу Иро́нии
для э́той суро́вой земли́.
Я дал ей владе́нья огро́мные:
пари́, усмеха́йся, шали́.

Зеве́са надме́нные до́чери,
ценя́ превосхо́дство своё,
каки́х бы там у́мниц ни ко́рчили –
не сто́ят гроша́ без неё.

1985

Francois Villon's Prayer

Oh Lord, while Earth's still spinning, while the sky is illumined still,
Give to each one what is lacking so his dreams can be fulfilled.
Give the sage more wisdom, the coward the means to flee;
To fortune's pet give more money and do not forget about me.

Oh Lord, while Earth's still spinning, and all fates are in your hand.
Give the thrill of power to those who can't wait to command,
Give big-hearted folks a respite, if just for a single day
Give to Cain repentance, and don't forget me, I pray.

Oh, Lord, I know you're almighty, that you are loving and wise
As soldiers who've been slaughtered believe they're in paradise.
As all those who've heard your soft message have put their trust in you
As we ourselves do trust you, though we know not twhat we do.

Oh, green-eyed God in heaven, you who all pain relieve,
While our Earth's still spinning, as she herself finds hard to believe;
While there is still time and fire, oh, Lord, will you answer this plea?
Give to each man, just a little, and do not forget about me.

1963
Translation by Lydia Stone and Vladimir Kovner

Моли́тва Франсуа́ Вийо́на

Пока́ Земля́ ещё ве́ртится, пока́ ещё я́рок свет,
Го́споди, дай же ты ка́ждому, чего́ у него́ нет:
му́дрому дай го́лову, трусли́вому дай коня́,
дай счастли́вому де́нег. И не забу́дь про меня́.

Пока́ Земля́ ещё ве́ртится, Го́споди, – твоя́ вла́сть!
дай рву́щемуся к вла́сти навла́ствоваться всла́сть,
дай переды́шку ще́дрому хоть до исхо́да дня.
Ка́ину дай раска́янье. И не забу́дь про меня́.

Я зна́ю: ты всё уме́ешь, я ве́рую в му́дрость твою́,
как ве́рит солда́т уби́тый, что он прожива́ет в раю́,
как ве́рит ка́ждое у́хо ти́хим реча́м твои́м,
как ве́руем и мы са́ми, не ве́дая, что твори́м!

Го́споди, мой Бо́же, зеленогла́зый мой!
Пока́ Земля́ ещё ве́ртится, и э́то ей стра́нно само́й,
пока́ ей ещё хвата́ет вре́мени и огня́.
дай же ты всем понемно́гу. И не забу́дь про меня́.

1963

Song about an Old, Sick, Tired King
who Set Off to Conquer Another Country,
and the Results of This

In fairy tale times, an old king once resolved to assault
The kingdom next door (for he thought the conditions propitious).
The queen packed a lunch for him (hoping he'd find it delicious),
Including tobacco; she even remembered the salt.

She gave him a kiss and she called him her darling, her pet.
Then smiling and looking him straight in the eye she commanded,
"Now beat them up good so a pacifist you won't be branded,
And seize all their cookies and bring them back home, don't forget."

The king went outside, where his army had massed in the yard:
Five lighthearted soldiers, five sad ones, one private first class.
The king said: "Be fearless, let's go out and kick our foe's ass!
We'll let nothing stop us, not even the press." They hurrahed.

Then they all saluted and after that said their goodbyes.
The king on the way there resolved to restructure his force.
His five gloomy soldiers he kept in the front line (of course),
While those who were cheerful were moved back to see to supplies.

It's hard to imagine, but victory went to the king,
Though all the sad soldiers had died while performing their duty.
The PFC traitor, what's more, wed an enemy beauty,
But bagfuls of cookies were captured and that's the main thing.

Let there be rejoicing, bands playing and all that good stuff,
My friends, don't be sad, there's no reason for people to cry.
For some did survive, and it makes sense sad soldiers should die.
Recall too, for all there never are cookies enough.

1961
Translation by Lydia Stone and Vladimir Kovner

Пе́сенка о ста́ром, больно́м, уста́лом короле́, кото́рый отпра́вился завоёвывать чужу́ю страну́, и о том, что из э́того получи́лось

В похо́д на чужу́ю страну́ собира́лся коро́ль.
Ему́ короле́ва мешо́к сухаре́й насуши́ла
И ста́рую ма́нтию так аккура́тно заши́ла,
Дала́ ему́ па́чку махо́рки и в тря́почке соль.

И ру́ки свои́ королю́ положи́ла на гру́дь,
Сказа́ла ему́, обласка́в его́ взо́ром лучи́стым:
«Полу́чше их бей, а не то́ прослывёшь пацифи́стом,
И пря́ников сла́дких отня́ть у врага́ не забу́дь.»

И ви́дит коро́ль – его́ во́йско стои́т средь двора́.
Пять гру́стных солда́т, пять весёлых солда́т и ефре́йтор.
Сказа́л им коро́ль: «Не страшны́ нам ни пре́сса, ни ве́тер,
Врага́ мы побьём, и с побе́дой придём, и ура́!»

Но вот отгреме́ло проща́льных рече́й торжество́.
В похо́де коро́ль свою́ а́рмию переина́чил:
Весёлых солда́т интенда́нтами сра́зу назна́чил,
А гру́стных оста́вил в солда́тах– «Аво́сь, ничего́».

Предста́вьте себе́, наступи́ли побе́дные дни.
Пять гру́стных солда́т не верну́лись из схва́тки вое́нной.
Ефре́йтор, мора́льно несто́йкий, жени́лся на пле́нной,
Но пря́ников це́лый мешо́к захвати́ли они́.

Игра́йте, орке́стры, звучи́те, и пе́сни и смех.
Мину́тной печа́ли не сто́ит, друзья́, предава́ться.
Ведь гру́стным солда́там нет смы́сла в живы́х остава́ться,
И пря́ников, кста́ти, всегда́ не хвата́ет на всех.

1961

A Swedish Spy
Bulat Okudzhava

1965. I was sent to perform in the Far East of Russia. I was not dying to go there, and did nothing to bring this about, but the Writers' Union for some reason really wanted it to happen. It was responding to some mysterious vibration shaking its mechanism, quite powerful at that time. I permitted myself to make all kinds of unreasonable stipulations. For example, I said that I refused to fly there and insisted on going by train. The organizers didn't object, indicating that whatever I wanted was fine and all my conditions would be met. If I wanted to go by train, they would arrange it – I could take a sleeper until the ends of the earth. But even this was not enough for me. Wouldn't this mean I would have to share a two-berth compartment with a roommate? In other words, for eight days some complete stranger would be torturing me with his snoring and his conversation, and might even drink himself into a stupor, contaminating my air with alcoholic fumes.

"Buy me two tickets," I said. "I want to be alone."

"No problem," they answered with a smile.

Finally everything was arranged. I received a pass that allowed me to travel to Vladivostok. (In those days this border city required special

Я – ШВЕ́ДСКИЙ ШПИО́Н

Була́т Окуджа́ва

Шестьдеся́т пя́тый год. Меня́ отправля́ют на Да́льний Восто́к с выступле́ниями. Я не рвусь туда́, никогда́ э́того не добива́лся, но Сою́з писа́телей как то чрезме́рно заинтересо́ван, кака́я то тайнственная вибра́ция сотряса́ет его́ механи́зм, в те го́ды доста́точно мо́щный. Я позволя́ю себе́ вся́кие капри́зы. Ну, наприме́р, говорю́, что самолётом не полечу́ – то́лько по желе́зной доро́ге. Организа́торы не возража́ют: пожа́луйста, как вам бу́дет уго́дно, нам все досту́пно, по́ездом – так по́ездом. Пое́дете в спа́льном ваго́не до са́мого са́мого... Но э́того мне ма́ло. Я ведь бу́ду в двуспа́льном купе́ не оди́н. Како́й нибудь незнако́мый тип бу́дет все во́семь дней истяза́ть меня́ хра́пом, разгово́рами, а мо́жет, бу́дет пить беспробу́дно и дыша́ть ви́нным перега́ром.

– Возьми́те мне два биле́та, – говорю́ я жёстко, – я хочу́ е́хать оди́н.

– Нет пробле́м, – улыба́ются они́.

Наконе́ц все офо́рмлено. Я получа́ю про́пуск на въезд во Владивосто́к. (В те го́ды э́тот приграни́чный го́род был на

permission.) I settled into my compartment. I made myself at home: after all, it would be a long trip. What a pleasure, to be alone! I hung up and arranged my things. The typewriter, paper, and pens went on the desk.

The conductor came in – a fellow with a red forelock and a wide smile – to ask me if I wanted tea. He brought me tea and pastries. His name was Pasha.

The train moved on. Night fell. I slept well. In the morning I went out into the corridor. Pasha passed by, but did not look at me.

"Good morning, Pasha."

He turned away and did not answer.

Well, I thought to myself in irritation, just another boor, and he had seemed so pleasant. Truly, he would not answer my questions, and if he did, he would look past me, so my desire to ask him anything soon passed. He did not offer me tea again. I did not want to lower myself so I went to the dining car and ate and drank to my heart's content.

I worked. The countryside outside the window was monotonous. Days passed. Vladivostok was getting close. On the last night, I was awakened by a knock at the door; it opened and an officer came inside.

"Travel-pass check."

I gave him my pass. He studied it for a long time.

"Passport," he said.

I handed him my passport. He was acting strangely. His movements were deliberate, his lips pursed. He examined every letter.

"What other documents do you have?"

I began to understand that something was wrong. And without speaking I did what he asked. I offered him my Writer Union's membership card, my trip orders, my military discharge papers.

He studied them for what seemed an eternity. Then he returned them, saluted and left, and I saw the red-headed Pasha mincing after him.

In the morning, as if nothing had happened, Pasha, smiling merrily, brought me tea and a package of pastries.

специа́льном режи́ме.) Забира́юсь в своё купе. Устра́иваюсь: е́хать ведь до́лго. Како́е сча́стье – я оди́н! Все разве́шиваю, расставля́ю. Пи́шущая маши́нка на сто́лике, бума́га, перо́...

Прихо́дит проводни́к. Ры́жий чу́бчик. Широ́кая улы́бка.

– Чайку́ не жела́ете?

Он прино́сит чай, пече́нье. Его́ зову́т Па́ша.

По́езд идёт. Спуска́ется ночь. Я хорошо́ высыпа́юсь. У́тром выхожу́ в коридо́р. Па́ша прохо́дит ми́мо. На меня́ не смо́трит.

– Здра́вствуйте, Па́ша.

Он отвора́чивается, отвора́чивается и не отвеча́ет.

Ну во́т, ду́маю я с раздраже́нием, очередно́й хам, а каза́лся таки́м сво́йским. И действи́тельно, он не отвеча́ет на мои́ вопро́сы, а е́сли и отвеча́ет, то гля́дя ми́мо меня́ и та́к, что жела́ние спра́шивать пропада́ет. Ча́ю бо́льше не предлага́ет. Мне не хо́чется унижа́ться. Хожу́ в ваго́н рестора́н и ем и пью ско́лько пожела́ю.

Мне рабо́тается. Пейза́ж за окно́м однообра́зен. Прохо́дят дни. Приближа́ется Владивосто́к. В после́днюю ночь, накану́не прие́зда, я просыпа́юсь от сту́ка в дверь, она́ тотча́с же открыва́ется, и вхо́дит офице́р:

– Прове́рка про́пусков.

Подаю́ ему́ про́пуск. Он до́лго его́ изуча́ет.

– Па́спорт, – говори́т он.

Протя́гиваю па́спорт. Он ведёт себя́ стра́нно. Движе́ния заме́дленны, гу́бы сжа́ты. Он вчи́тывается в ка́ждую бу́кву.

– Каки́е ещё есть докуме́нты?

Я понима́ю: что́ то не та́к. И мо́лча выполня́ю его́ распоряже́ния. Предлага́ю ему́ писа́тельскую кни́жку, командиро́вочное удостовере́ние, вое́нный биле́т...

Он изуча́ет их до́лго до́лго. Пото́м возвраща́ет, козыря́ет и ухо́дит, и я ви́жу, как ры́жий Па́ша семени́т за ним сле́дом.

У́тром ка́к ни в чём не быва́ло, ра́достно улыба́ясь, Па́ша прино́сит мне чай и па́чку пече́нья.

He sat down across from me and I learned the following.

The day I left Moscow, all the Moscow train stations had received a secret notice that a certain Swede was traveling from Moscow in an unknown direction without the required special permission. Task forces conducted searches at all stations. Conductors on all trains were ordered to keep everyone who seemed suspicious under surveillance and to report on them regularly. A spy could not be permitted to operate freely.

When he received this assignment, Pasha immediately reported that there was a suspicious fellow in his car. This fellow was travelling alone in a compartment on two tickets, never left the train when it stopped at stations, and spent all day banging on his typewriter.

He described him as medium height, thin, black hair, a mustache – in other words, a typical Swede.

Pasha's information was received with near salacious pleasure and, since the concept of "Caucasian nationality" had not yet entered public consciousness in those years, they immediately decided that this individual was a Swede. They put me under meticulous surveillance for the entire eight-day period, and needless to say were highly disappointed when they checked my documents.

Pasha told me this while smiling from ear to ear. "On the very first day, I told them to check your documents. Why drag things out for eight days? But they answered that they were the professionals, and who was I to try and teach them their job? But I, too, was convinced that you were a Swedish spy." And he roared with laughter. He was so nice, so friendly, so vigilant, that Pasha.

First published in Russian: 1996
Translation by Lydia Stone

И садится напротив меня, и я узнаю следующее.

В день моего отъезда из Москвы все московские вокзалы получили секретное извещение о том, что некий швед выехал из Москвы в неизвестном направлении без специального на то разрешения. Опергруппы на всех вокзалах принялись за поиски. По всем поездам команда: проводники обязаны следить за всем подозрительным и регулярно докладывать. Шпион не должен действовать безнаказанно.

Получив задание, Паша тут же сообщил, что в его вагоне находится подозрительный тип: едет один в купе по двум билетам, на остановках не выходит, целый день стучит на машинке.

Роста среднего. Худой. Чёрный чубчик, чёрные усики. Типичный швед.

Донесение Паши выслушали с вожделением, а так как в те годы понятие «лицо кавказской национальности» было не в ходу, сразу догадались, что речь идёт о шведе. Все восемь дней тщательно следили и, конечно, крайне огорчились, проверив документы...

– Я им в первый день сказал, мол, проверьте документы, чего восемь дней то тянуть, – говорит Паша, улыбаясь во весь рот, – а они мне, мол, мы профессионалы, и ты нас не учи, понятно?.. А я тоже думал, что вы шведский шпион! – и хохочет. Такой милый, свойский, такой бдительный. Паша.

Murderer
Bulat Okudzhava

Less than a year after I was taken for a Swedish spy, something incredible happened. The Writers' Union invited my wife and I to join a group of Russians on a planned excursion to Sweden. I could not believe it was really going to happen – my first time in capitalist Europe! – but it seemed about to. The group was a small one: eight writers and their wives.

Sixteen people, and I was to be one of them. Zhenya Yevtushenko[1] had already visited the West more than once, but he was delighted on my behalf and winked at me encouragingly. But suddenly, just before we were to leave, I found out that I had been crossed off the list. I nearly wept. I hurried over to see Ilyin – the KGB general who was in charge of the Moscow writers. He nodded at the ceiling and said that they had changed their minds about me.

"It is your own fault," he said sadly. "You sing all kinds of ditties that irritate the authorities."

"But how could this have happened?" I sighed with despair. "I was so happy about it... and my wife... You know, I was a front line combatant!"

---

1. The famous poet and writer Yevgeny Yevtushenko.

УБИ́ЙЦА

Була́т Окуджа́ва

Не прошло́ и го́да, как случи́лось невероя́тное: Сою́з писа́телей организова́л туристи́ческую гру́ппу для пое́здки в Шве́цию и меня́ с жено́й включи́ли то́же! Я не ве́рил: впервы́е в капиталисти́ческую Евро́пу! Сверши́лось! Гру́ппа была́ ма́ленькая: во́семь писа́телей с жёнами.

Шестна́дцать челове́к. И я среди́ них! Же́ня Евтуше́нко на За́паде уже́ быва́л, и неоднокра́тно, но ра́довался за меня́ и подми́гивал поощри́тельно. И вдруг перед са́мым отъе́здом вы́яснилось, что меня́ из спи́ска вы́черкнули!.. Я чу́ть не запла́кал. Я побежа́л к Ильину́ – генера́лу КГБ, кото́рый руководи́л моско́вскими писа́телями. Он кивну́л на потоло́к и сказа́л, что в отноше́нии меня́ переду́мали.

– Сам винова́т, – сказа́л он с гру́стью, – поёшь вся́кие пе́сенки, раздража́ешь нача́льство...

– Да ка́к же так?! – вы́дохнул я с отча́янием. – Я был так рад... и жена́... Я же фронтови́к!..

"That is irrelevant," he said. "You need to mend your ways, and next time... "

At this point, Yevtushenko, much upset, entered the room. He nodded to the general and sat down opposite him without being asked, and said glumly:

"Viktor Nikolayevich, the fact is that all of Sweden is waiting with bated breath for his (he nodded at me) arrival. There has been all kinds of media frenzy about him..." (A chill ran down my spine – it was the first I had heard of anything of the kind.) "If he doesn't show up, it will cause an international scandal. I do not know who is at fault, but it will be impossible to explain. I will assume all responsibility for him. Everything was all set, and now this happens!"

Ilyin listened, nodded, and looked over at me. I was sitting there feeling neither dead nor alive. Something inside of me felt like it had broken. There had been so many things like this in my life – humiliating insults or insulting humiliations, or both together, and so many of them. "Never mind," I thought to myself. "This won't kill me."

"Well, OK" said the general, "OK, I will take responsibility, OK, what the hell... "

After we left, I asked Zhenya, "What was that you were saying about a media frenzy?"

"What are you talking about?"

"Well, you said... "

"Oh, that," he waved his hand and laughed.

The next day on Mokhovaya Street, in some kind of government office, I cannot remember which, they gave us a briefing. I listened very carefully; I didn't miss a single word. I took it all to heart. At the end, an official with cold eyes summarized what had been said:

"Remember, you are going to a capitalist country. This world teems with spies and saboteurs. Remember that hippies are especially dangerous."

"Who are they?" I asked, fearfully.

— Ничего, — сказал он неумолимо, — наладь все эти дела, и в следующий раз...

И тут вошёл обеспокоенный Евтушенко. Он кивнул генералу, сел напротив без приглашения и сказал мрачно:

— Виктор Николаевич, дело в том, что вся Швеция с замиранием сердца ждёт его, — (он кивнул в мою сторону), — приезда. У них очень большой ажиотаж... — (Я похолодел: впервые я слышал о себе такое.) — Если он не приедет, разразится международный скандал. Я не знаю, по чьей вине, но объяснить будет невозможно... В конце концов, я беру на себя всю ответственность... Ведь все было готово, и вдруг такое!..

Ильин слушал, кивал, поглядывал на меня, а я сидел ни жив ни мёртв, и что то такое во мне оборвалось, а в жизни моей было так много подобного — оскорбительных унижений или унизительных оскорблений или и того и другого, да в таком количестве... Ничего, подумал я, не сдохну.

— Ну ладно, — вдруг сказал генерал, — ладно, беру на себя ответственность, ладно, черт с вами...

Когда мы вышли, я спросил Женю:

— Что это ты говорил насчёт ажиотажа?

— Какого ажиотажа? — не понял он.

— Ну, ты говорил... — сказал я.

— А а, — махнул он рукой и засмеялся.

На следующий день на Моховой в каком то учреждении, сейчас уж и не помню в каком, с нами провели собеседование. Я слушал очень внимательно, не пропускал ни единого слова, был крайне возбуждён. В заключение чиновник с холодными глазами суммировал сказанное:

— Запомните: вы едете в капиталистическую страну. В этом мире кишат шпионы и диверсанты. Запомните: особенно опасны хиппи...

— Кто это такие?! — спросил я, теряя сознание.

"They are," said the official, "young people with long hair, drug addicts and murderers."

My happiness died. My stress levels peaked.

And so we went to Sweden.

In Stockholm it was sunny and warm. The city was gorgeous. Oh, if only it had not been for the recurring thought about the dangers it concealed! If only it weren't for the terror that shackled our souls! A clean and comfortable capital, friendly service, an elegant and unaccustomed dinner; but also the constant chill, the shivering at the thought of the danger we were in. From the fourth floor window we could see the clean street, the unconstrained, well-dressed passersby, and the clean Mercedeses and Volvos.

But that was from the fourth floor.

"But just try to go out there, and something awful will immediately happen," I said in a whisper.

My wife nodded. There were no group activities planned for the first day. Suddenly my wife frowned and said, also in a whisper:

"Well, damn it, are we going to sit here like prisoners? What the hell!" And she made for the door.

I dragged myself after her. We spoke only in whispers. The elevator was full of people. They smiled at each other and laughed, speaking in Swedish, English and French. While we...

We continued to whisper and to feel contempt for ourselves for doing so. And when we arrived at the lobby, my wife said loudly and clearly:

"Enough of this! I have decided that either we must act like the Swedes or lock ourselves in the bathroom for the entire duration of the trip."

"What do I have to do with spies and saboteurs? Enough!" We went out onto the noisy street.

"Look at their faces," she said, "How they laugh, how they move. Fine spies they make."

"Shh, shh... " I whispered and looked around fearfully.

— Это, — сказал чиновник, — молодые люди с длинными волосами, наркоманы и убийцы...

Радость моя померкла. Напряжение достигло апогея.

И мы поехали в Швецию.

В Стокгольме было солнечно и жарко. Город был прекрасен. О, если бы не назойливая мысль о таящихся в нем опасностях! Если бы не страх, сковывающий наши души!.. Удобная и чистая гостиница, доброжелательное обслуживание, изысканный непривычный ужин, но постоянный озноб, дрожь по коже и мысли об опасности. Из окна четвёртого этажа мы видели чистую улицу и раскованных, хорошо одетых прохожих и чистенькие «мерседесы» и «вольво».

Но это с четвёртого этажа.

— А попробуй выйди туда — и сразу что нибудь случится, — шёпотом сказал я.

Жена кивнула. На первый день никаких коллективных мероприятий не было. Вдруг жена моя поморщилась и сказала мне тоже шёпотом:

— Ну что, так и будем сидеть взаперти? Какого черта!.. — и вдруг пошла к двери.

Я потащился за ней. Мы общались только шёпотом. В лифте набилось полно народу. Они улыбались друг другу, хохотали, и слышалась шведская, английская и французская речь. А мы?

А мы перешёптывались и презирали сами себя. И когда спустились и вышли в холл, жена произнесла громко и отчётливо:

— Хватит! Я подумала: или как шведы, или закрыться в туалете на весь срок поездки!

Какое я имею отношение к шпионам, а тем более — к диверсантам?! Хватит!.. Мы вышли на шумную улицу.

— Посмотри на их лица, — сказала она, — как они смеются, как движутся... Ничего себе шпионы!

— Тише, тише, — шепнул я и напряжённо оглянулся.

She did not answer. It was stifling. Then she said bitterly, "here we are hanging around the hotel. We might as well go back to Moscow. God! How hot it is."

And then I saw a Coca-Cola machine right next to the entrance. We went over to it. I put in my coin, but nothing happened. I started to push various buttons, but it did no good.

I got out another coin. Suddenly on my left I saw a huge, hairy arm. It was reaching for my coin! I raised my head and my blood ran cold: next to me stood an enormously tall hippie with hair down to his shoulders. He muttered something and reached for my coin.

"Let him have it," whispered my wife, who had turned pale. "For God's sake, give it to him."

"Well," I thought to myself, "the ominous warning was correct after all."

"Give it to him," my wife whispered desperately. "Who knows what he is capable of?"

And the hippie muttered something and continued to reach for the coin. I gave it to him. I felt humiliated.

"Could it really be," I thought, "that he is capable of murdering someone for such a trifle?" With my eyes I indicated to my wife that she should go back inside the hotel. But she was frozen with fear. I waited tensely to see what he would do next. He was sure to pull some terrible trick – I hadn't even asked for his help – and even if I had asked him, he was not obligated to help. He could simply... why did he have to? He could say, "Get out of here!" And I would go...

The hippie dropped the coin into a slot in the machine, pushed a button, and an icy bottle fell into his palm. He removed the cap and gave a huge smile. He gave the bottle to my wife with a bow. And left, but not before he had waved goodbye.

First published in Russian: 1996
Translation by Lydia Stone

Она́ умо́лкла. Бы́ло ду́шно. Пото́м сказа́ла с го́речью:

– Вот пото́пчемся пе́ред гости́ницей, и мо́жно в Москву́ возвраща́ться... Го́споди, как ду́шно!..

И ту́т я уви́дел пря́мо у са́мого подъе́зда – автома́ты с ко́ка ко́лой. Мы подошли́ к ним. Я опусти́л моне́ту, но автома́т не сраба́тал. Я стал нажима́ть каки́е то кно́пки – никако́го то́лку.

Доста́л другу́ю моне́ту. Вдруг уви́дел сле́ва от себя́ грома́дную волоса́тую ру́ку. Она́ тяну́лась к мое́й моне́те! Я по́дня́л го́лову и похолоде́л: ря́дом со мной стоя́л высо́ченный хи́ппи с волоса́ми до плеч. Он бормота́л что то и тяну́лся к мое́й моне́те.

– Отда́й ему́, отда́й, – прошепта́ла бле́дная моя́ жена́, – да отда́й же!

Ну во́т, поду́мал я, сбыли́сь злове́щие проро́чества.

– Лу́чше отда́й, – шепну́ла жена́ с отча́янием, – он на все спосо́бен!

А хи́ппи что то бубни́л и продолжа́л тяну́ться к моне́те. И я отдал её ему́. Я был уни́жен.

Неуже́ли, поду́мал я, он спосо́бен уби́ть из за тако́й ерунды́?! Я показа́л жене́ глаза́ми на две́рь в гости́ницу, но она́ пребыва́ла в столбняке́. Я напряжённо следи́л за хи́ппи. Я ждал подво́ха:

без э́того не могло́ быть... Я же не проси́л его́... А е́сли бы да́же попроси́л, он не обя́зан... Он мог про́сто... почему́ он до́лжен? Он мог сказа́ть: «Да иди́ ты!..» И я бы пошёл...

Хи́ппи опусти́л моне́тку в щёлочку автома́та, нажа́л каку́ю то кно́пку, и ледяна́я буты́лка впры́гнула ему́ на ладо́нь. Он сорва́л про́бку, и лицо́ его́ расплыло́сь в улы́бке. Он протяну́л буты́лку мое́й жене! И при э́том поклони́лся! И ушёл... «Бай бай...»

Greetings, Your Majesty

Bulat Okudzhava

After perestroika I visited Sweden again. I strolled through Stockholm, without fear. The Russian fear mongers had disappeared as though they had never existed. This time, I remembered the earlier years with a smile, blushing for my actions, and glad of the new situation.

By the way, I remembered a few more episodes associated with the previous tourist excursion I had taken many years before.

In the past, a time when I never would have imagined it would ever be possible for me to visit Sweden, I made the acquaintance in Moscow with Hans, a Swedish correspondent and writer. We sometimes got together to talk. He was a cheerful, intelligent young man, who was never able to reconcile the sadness of my poems and songs with the nervous bustle of my inflamed mind. After a while his Moscow posting came to an end. He returned to his homeland, and soon after that I had the honor of getting a look at the capitalist world for the first time.

And in Stockholm, after the incident with the hippie, when I had already learned a thing or two – though not everything, of course – he tracked me down and invited my wife and I to have supper at his home.

ЗДРА́ВСТВУЙТЕ, ВА́ШЕ ВЕЛИ́ЧЕСТВО!

Була́т Окуджа́ва

Уже́ по́сле нача́ла перестро́йки я сно́ва побыва́л в Шве́ции. Я гуля́л по Стокго́льму. Я ничего́ не боя́лся. Пуга́льщики за́мерли, сло́вно их никогда́ и не́ было. Все предше́ствующие го́ды я тепе́рь вспомина́л с улы́бкой, красне́л за себя́ того́ и ра́довался но́вым обстоя́тельствам.

Кста́ти, вспо́мнил ещё не́сколько эпизо́дов, свя́занных с той, тепе́рь уже́ да́вней, пое́здкой тури́стом.

Тогда́, ещё не представля́я себе́, что смогу́ пое́хать в Шве́цию, я познако́мился в Москве́ с шве́дским корреспонде́нтом и писа́телем Ха́нсом. Мы иногда́ обща́лись. Он был весёлый, у́мный молодо́й челове́к, кото́рый ника́к не мог совмести́ть гру́сть мои́х стихо́в и пе́сен с кра́сной суето́й в моем воспалённом мозгу́. Зате́м срок его́ пребыва́ния в Москве́ зако́нчился, он уе́хал к себе́ на ро́дину, а тут вско́ре и мне вы́пала честь впервы́е загляну́ть в капиталисти́ческий мир.

И вот в Стокго́льме, уже́ по́сле исто́рии с хи́ппи, когда́ я уже́ ко́е что уясни́л, коне́чно не до конца́, он разыска́л меня́ и пригласи́л нас с жено́й в свой дом поу́жинать.

He lived in a two story apartment. I had never seen one before. An elegant table had been laid downstairs. Everything was delicious, noisy and cheerful. A number of anecdotes were told in which my countrymen were portrayed in a humorous light. Hans was great. Suddenly, he proposed to give me a tour of the upstairs of his apartment. My mood was good. My head was spinning slightly. I nodded and followed him. I was impressed by his living quarters. Of course, I thought to myself, he is a correspondent – a wealthy man. All of a sudden, a suspicion entered my head – what if he is really a common intelligence agent? He has invited me to his home and now is taking me upstairs to the second floor. And what will happen when we get there? Now, I thought, he will begin to persuade me to, er, collaborate.

My feet turned to lead. I followed him like a prisoner. He turned back towards me and smiled. I knew all about such smiles! We climbed the stairs. I drew in my head. We knew all about it. My intoxication vanished.

"Well, here we are," he said. "This is my office." I could make out something through the fog.

"And this is the bedroom," he said, opening the next door.

"Now it will start," I thought, and froze in my tracks.

"What's the matter?" he asked. "You don't seem to be very interested."

"Well, I've seen bedrooms before," I muttered. "Why don't we go back downstairs?" And I waited for him to begin on his speech.

"OK," he agreed easily. "Next we are going to have crabs. Do you like crabs?

I had never tasted crabs.

"Of course," I said, and began to breathe more easily.

Several days later, another ridiculous incident occurred. Zhenya Yevtushenko, who had long been a frequent visitor of Europe, had taken me under his wing and was trying as hard as he could to make me comfortable with the ways of the West. As part of this campaign, he had convinced a mutual acquaintance, a Swedish publisher, to organize a trip to a striptease club. When all had been arranged, I exulted internally but affectedly

Это была двухэтажная квартира. Я таких никогда не видел! Внизу был накрыт изысканный стол. Было вкусно, шумно и весело. Звучали анекдоты, в которых мои соотечественники представали в комическом свете. Ханс был прекрасен. Вдруг он предложил мне посмотреть второй этаж его квартиры. Настроение было хорошее. Голова немного кружилась. Я кивнул и двинулся за ним. Меня поразило устройство этой квартиры. Конечно, подумал я, корреспондент – это же богатый человек! Внезапно в мозгу возникло подозрение: а что если он обыкновенный разведчик?! И пригласил меня в свой дом и теперь ведёт меня... на второй этаж!.. А там что? И теперь, подумал я, он начнёт уговаривать меня... ну, это... сотрудничать...

Я переступал деревянными ногами. Я шёл за ним, как пленник. Он оборачивался и улыбался. Знаю я ваши улыбки! Мы поднялись. Я втянул голову в плечи. Знаем мы... Хмель выветрился.

– Ну вот, – сказал он, – это мой кабинет. Что то такое проступило сквозь туман.

– А это спальня, – сказал он, приоткрыв следующую дверь.

Вот сейчас! – подумал я и остановился.

– Ну что? – спросил он. – Тебе, кажется, не интересно?

– Да что я, спален не видел? – пробормотал я. – Давай, пожалуй, вернёмся, – и ждал, что он сейчас то и начнёт...

– Хорошо, – легко согласился он, – сейчас нам подадут крабов. Ты любишь крабов?

Я никогда не ел крабов.

– Конечно, – сказал я, и дышать стало полегче...

... Через несколько дней случилась ещё одна нелепость. Женя Евтушенко, давно ставший завсегдатаем в Европе, очень меня опекал и старался всеми силами приобщить к Западу. И вот он уговорил нашего общего знакомого – шведского издателя – устроить посещение ночного клуба со стриптизом! Когда все было решено, я внутренне возликовал, но деланно поморщился, ибо одна моя половина была,

wrinkled up my nose, since half of me was, naturally, filled with curiosity, greedy for discovery, and charmed by the accessibility of a mystery, while the second half, blushing, burned over the slow fire of honorable self-righteousness. That explained the grimace of disgust.

We were seated at a table right in front of the stage. The lights went out. Zhenya and my wife were sitting opposite me. He had told her something, and now she was looking at me with an expression of great interest. The music began.

A woman in a short starched skirt, long-legged with a large, sumptuous chest – covered for the time being with a lace blouse – appeared on the stage. "Well, now," I thought. "What is so shocking about this?" The woman began to dance.

"Is this it?" I asked nonchalantly.

The woman threw off her blouse. Zhenya came over to me.

"I have to warn you," he whispered intensely. "She is going to strip naked, and then come into the audience, and possibly sit on your lap."

"What?!" I nearly shouted.

"Well, that's their routine," he said, "I know... But don't even think of pushing her away or anything of the sort... Understand? The last thing we need is to make a scene... "

And he went back to his seat and again exchanged glances with my wife.

The dancer continued to disrobe. First she threw off her brassiere, disclosing breasts of mediocre elasticity, which swayed in time to the music. Then her fluffy skirt flew off like an autumn leaf. The only thing left was something also resembling a leaf – a fig leaf.

I waited. I was so tense that I did not hear the music. Any minute now, she would come down into the audience. But the music stopped and sparse applause was heard. The light on the stage went out. I was saved. My heart beat desperately. My wife and Zhenya laughed.

Yes, this really happened. And now twenty years have flown by, and I am again in Stockholm. I am riding in a car. It is a sunny midday in autumn. Suddenly the car stops, and I see that all the cars in front of

есте́ственно, перепо́лнена любопы́тством, жа́ждой откры́тий, очаро́вана досту́пностью та́йны, но втора́я, кра́сная, горе́ла на ме́дленном огне́ заслуженного ха́нжества. Вот и грима́са отвраще́ния.

Мы за́няли сто́лик перед са́мой сце́ной. Вспы́хнул свет. Же́ня и моя жена́ сиде́ли напро́тив меня́. Он что то говори́л ей, и она́ погля́дывала на меня́ с больши́м интере́сом. Гря́нула му́зыка.

На сце́не появи́лась же́нщина в коро́ткой крахма́льной ю́бочке, длиннoно́гая, с большо́й пы́шной гру́дью, поку́да скры́той под кружевно́й блу́зочкой. Ну́ и что? – поду́мал я, скажи́те пожа́луйста, не́видаль... Же́нщина начала́ пританцо́вывать.

– И э́то все? – спроси́л я небре́жно. Же́нщина сбро́сила с себя́ блу́зочку. Женя подскочи́л ко мне.

– Я до́лжен тебя́ предупреди́ть, – горячо́ прошепта́л он, – сейча́с она́ обнажи́тся, спу́стится в зал и, возмо́жно, ся́дет тебе́ на коле́ни...

– Что?! – чу́ть не кри́кнул я.

– Ну, у них так при́нято, – сказа́л он, – я зна́ю... Но ты не вздума́й её оттолкну́ть и́ли ещё что нибу́дь... Ты по́нял? Не на́до сканда́лов...

И сно́ва усе́лся на своё ме́сто, и сно́ва перегляну́лся с мое́й жено́й.

Танцо́вщица продолжа́ла раздева́ться. Снача́ла ски́нула бюстга́льтер, и обнажи́лись не о́чень упру́гие груди, колы́шущиеся в такт му́зыке. Зате́м, сло́вно осе́нний лист, слете́ла с неё пы́шная юбчо́нка. Еди́нственное, что оста́лось, – э́то не́что, напомина́ющее фи́говый листо́к...

Я ждал. Я так напря́гся, что не слы́шал му́зыки. Сейча́с она́ сойдёт со сце́ны... Но му́зыка умо́лкла, и раздали́сь жи́дкие аплодисме́нты. Свет на сце́не пога́с. Я был спасён. Се́рдце би́лось отча́янно. Моя жена́ и Же́ня посме́ивались.

Да, все э́то бы́ло. И вот пролете́ло два́дцать лет, и я сно́ва в Стокго́льме. Я е́ду в автомоби́ле. Со́лнечный осе́нний по́лдень. Вдруг маши́на остана́вливается, и я ви́жу, что и всё иду́щие впереди́

us have also stopped. A traffic jam. There are no traffic lights. There is some kind of movement on the cross street ahead. I see a squadron of horsemen in old-fashioned uniforms, somewhere between hussars and ulans. They slowly and majestically cross in front of us, and are followed by – just imagine! – an old-fashioned open landau. That's right, a landau, and in it is a woman. I gasped; it was the Queen of Sweden! Oh – such things do not happen every day!

I leapt out of the car and ran to the crossroad, as fast as I could to get there in time. I stood right on the corner. I was wearing a coat and cap, and felt overheated. The landau drew even with me.

Sylvia, the Queen of Sweden – all beauty and dignity – was sitting on a leather throne. And I watched as she turned her head and looked at me, she virtually stared.

I wanted to bow to her but she had already turned away. Before I even had a chance to feel sorry, she looked right at me again, for the second time. And again she turned away.

Upon returning to my hotel, filled to the brim with all kinds of exalted feelings, I dared to write her a short message.

> *Your Majesty!*
>
> *I was standing at the very edge of the sidewalk. You passed by and looked fixedly at me twice. I am not a Monarchist, Your Majesty, but this made an extremely powerful impression on me, and I will remember it for the rest of my life!*

The next day they brought me her reply.

> *Dear sir!*
>
> *I remember: you were indeed standing at the edge of the sidewalk, and I looked fixedly at you twice, because when I came up to you, you, dear sir, neglected to remove your cap.*

First published in Russian: 1996
Translation by Lydia Stone

маши́ны останови́лись то́же. Зато́р. Светофо́ра нет. Впереди́ на у́лице, пересека́ющей на́шу, како́е то движе́ние. Я ви́жу эскадро́н вса́дников в стари́нных одея́ниях: то ли гуса́ры, то ли ула́ны. Они́ ме́дленно, торже́ственно пересека́ют наш путь, а за ни́ми, вы то́лько предста́вьте себе́, за ни́ми – стари́нное откры́тое ландо́, да да, ландо́, и в нем – же́нская фигу́ра. Я а́хнул: э́то была́ короле́ва Шве́ции! Ах, ведь не ка́ждый день случа́ется тако́е!

Я ки́нулся из маши́ны и побежа́л, побежа́л туда́, к перекрёстку, скоре́й, скоре́й, успе́ть бы... Встал на са́мом углу́. Стою́, сгора́я. На мне плащ и ке́пка. Ландо́ поравня́лось со мной.

Короле́ва Шве́ции, Си́львия, вся – красота́ и досто́инство, восседа́ет на ко́жаном тро́не! И я ви́жу, как она́ повора́чивает свою́ короле́вскую го́лову и всма́тривается в меня́, всма́тривается...

Я хоте́л ей поклони́ться, но она́ уже́ отверну́лась. Не успе́л я огорчи́ться, как она́ сно́ва взгляну́ла на меня́! Второ́й раз! И вновь отверну́лась.

Вороти́вшись в гости́ницу, я, перепо́лненный вся́кими возвы́шенными чу́вствами, рискну́л написа́ть ей коро́тенькое посла́ние.

«Ва́ше Вели́чество!

Я стоя́л на краю́ тротуа́ра. Вы проезжа́ли ми́мо и два ра́за внима́тельно посмотре́ли на меня́. Я не монархи́ст, Ва́ше Вели́чество, но мне бы́ло кра́йне прия́тно, и я навсегда́ запо́мню э́тот день!» На сле́дующий день мне вручи́ли от неё отве́т!

«Ми́лостивый госуда́рь!

Я по́мню: вы действи́тельно стоя́ли на краю́ тротуа́ра, и я два ра́за внима́тельно на вас посмотре́ла, потому́ что, когда́ я поравня́лась с ва́ми, вы, ми́лостивый госуда́рь, не сня́ли ке́пку».